CHRISTMAS OF LOVE

A LONG VALLEY ROMANCE NOVELLA - BOOK 5

ERIN WRIGHT

WRIGHT'S READS

To the teenage me:
I'm glad you didn't give up that day in the music closet

CHAPTER 1

IVY

DECEMBER, 2017

*W*ELL, this party was exactly as exciting as Ivy McLain thought it was going to be.

Which was to say, not very exciting at all.

Of course, this was Sawyer, Idaho. What else could she expect?

She sighed. Only this, unfortunately. A bunch of old farmers, standing around and jawing about how their crops didn't bring in enough money and there wasn't enough water this past year, or maybe there was *too* much water, and the combine broke down in the field again…

It was enough to make Ivy's head hurt. Why people intentionally chose to live this way was beyond her. Especially the cold part. She shivered, pulling her woefully inadequate jacket tighter around herself. *Ugh.* A little over two weeks before Christmas in Sawyer freakin' Idaho. She should be grateful it wasn't snowing, but she couldn't find it in herself to be that saintly.

It was too cold to be grateful *or* saintly.

Her mom looked up from her discussion with Mrs. Frank about plans for next year's garden, and waved. Ivy smiled as cheerfully as she could – which was to say, not cheerfully at all – and huffed out a breath. If she didn't love her parents so much, she never would've made herself come back here. Thank God it was just a weekend visit. To actually *live* in Sawyer again…

Another shiver ran through her – from disgust or cold, she couldn't tell – and she spun on her heel to head towards the refreshment table. She'd make herself some hot cocoa and—

"Oof!" she gasped, when she ran into a brick wall.

She looked up to see…

Well, the cutest brick wall she'd ever laid eyes on. The phrase "tall, dark, and handsome" was definitely appropriate. Thick brown hair just long enough to run her fingers through, and the most piercing emerald green eyes she'd ever had the pleasure to see. Whiplash quick, he reached out a hand to steady her, gripping her elbow to keep her upright.

"Howdy," he said, pushing his cowboy hat a little further up on his head. In his hand was a mug of mulled apple cider.

An *empty* mug of mulled apple cider, because she'd spilled it all over him with her clumsiness.

The world froze as she realized what she'd done. Dammit all, she was a waitress! She knew how to navigate in tight spots. What on earth was she doing, running people over like that? A painful silence stretched between them, a chasm as she stared at the damage she'd wreaked.

And then the dam broke, and the words came tumbling out.

"So sorry!" she gasped, looking at his jacket, covered in a brown liquid that was now dripping off onto the frozen ground. "So, so sorry. I wasn't watching where I was going and then you were there and...let me help clean you up. It's the least I can do." Not waiting for his response, she began dragging him towards the refreshment table, thankfully only a few feet away. She'd get him cleaned up and on his way, and then she'd run and hide in her parent's broom closet.

Preferably for the next year or so.

"No worries!" he said with a low chuckle as he hurried along behind her. She stopped abruptly at the table and began grabbing the paper towels. "This jacket needs to be dry cleaned anyway," he continued. "Kept meaning to take it on over to the Wash 'N Spin, but haven't had—"

Which is when she started patting his face dry, and he had to shut up. *Dammit, dammit, dammit.* She'd gotten apple cider everywhere. How on earth did she get it on his earlobe?! She was patting him dry and trying really hard to ignore his strong jaw covered with a light dusting of dark brown hair and green eyes and—

Just get this done already, Ivy!

Her pats were coming a little slower, though, as she got caught up in his gaze. They were only inches apart from each other, and sure, her hands were filled with dirty paper towels, and sure, his jacket was sticky to the touch from the cider, but in that moment?

None of that mattered.

All she could do was stare at him. She caught her lower lip between her teeth, her breath uneven.

"My name is Austin Bishop," he said, breaking the silence between them. "And yours is?"

Right. Name.

She probably should've thought to introduce herself before she put her hands all over his body, but better late than never, right?

"Ivy McLain," she said, proud that she could get her name out at all. She sounded breathless, but she *was* breathless, so there wasn't much to be done about that.

"I thought you looked like Iris," he said, with what was possibly the cutest grin she'd ever seen on a man's face.

"People say I look like her," Ivy said with a shrug, happy to note that her voice didn't sound quite as breathless as it had before. "I don't see it, personally."

"You don't see…" His voice trailed off and he cocked an eyebrow at her in disbelief. "You two could be twins," he said bluntly.

Ivy threw her head back and laughed. It was sweet of him to say, of course. And she wasn't going to be coy and demure and say that it wasn't true – even though it really wasn't – in an attempt to get him to give her more compliments.

But everyone knew that Iris was the prettier of the two, and there was no use pretending otherwise.

"So why the plant names?" Austin asked after her chuckles had died down a bit. His gaze was as intense as ever, like he was trying to memorize every curve, every freckle, every laugh wrinkle on her face. It was disconcerting to have someone look at her so…intently.

She tried not to read too much into it, though. He probably looked at everyone that way.

She shrugged. "My parents wanted us girls to remember 'our roots,' so they named us after plants. Mostly what ended up happening was they couldn't keep our names straight. I kid you not – I thought my name was Iris-Ivy for the longest time."

He chuckled, and a warmth spread through her that belied the brisk winter temperatures. She wanted to lean into him again, but this time, not be blotting up spilled apple cider. She wanted—

"Oh, there you are!"

The voice cut through the cold air like a whip – slicing through Ivy's heart and sending spasms of pain through her. *No, not her. She can't be here! Iris promised me she wouldn't invite—*

And then Tiffany was draping herself over Austin, practically climbing up his side. Tiffany sent Ivy a sickeningly sweet smile that didn't even vaguely reach her eyes, as she looked her up and down. Dismissing her, Tiffany turned back to Austin. "I didn't realize you'd be here, darlin'," she cooed. "I tried calling you about going to the ice skating show tomorrow night, but you didn't answer." She ran her fingers up his chest and to his face, bopping him on the nose playfully. If she was going to get any closer to him, she'd have to strip naked to do it.

Ivy began backing up, mumbling something that could've been, "Have a good time," or "Good food tonight," or "I hope you eat bugs and die…"

Really, it was quite mumbled, and even she wasn't sure what she said, and then she was spinning on her heel and heading towards the house, the dirtied paper towels still in her hands. She began wringing them in her hands as she walked.

"Austin and Tiffany?" she muttered under her breath as she stalked, blinded by rage as she went. "Tiffany?!" She could forgive him for anyone but Tiffany.

Okay, maybe not Ezzy, either.

But anyone but Tiffany or Ezzy, she could understand. But those two...they just didn't seem his type.

Not that she knew his type. She barely knew his name. But floozy, bitchy girls didn't seem like they should be anyone's type, if you asked her.

Not that anyone had, of course.

She tossed the dirty paper towels into a trashcan as she passed, and then stormed into the kitchen, muttering as she went. "Damn Tiffany, always ruining – Iris!" she yelped in surprise when she spotted her sister at the sink. Beautiful as ever, but a little more fragile than she used to be, Iris turned and shot her a smile.

Ivy scowled. Her sister had promised not to invite those two to the party. "You would not believe who is here!" she announced as she headed for the fruit platter on the counter. Yum – honeycrisp apples. They were her fav, and really only available in the fall and early winter. Which made them an even bigger treat when she could get her hands on them. She snatched one up and began crunching on it as she paced her parent's small kitchen.

Iris grabbed another potato and gave it a light scrub. "Yeah?" she prompted. She looked like she was in the middle of making the infamous McLain potato salad, which was awesome. If Ivy was going to be stuck in Long Valley for a weekend, she might as well enjoy something amazing to eat.

"Tiffany and Ezzy! You didn't invite them, did you?" Ivy asked around a mouthful of apple.

Iris turned, and without a word, sent Ivy a death glare.

That death glare. The patented Iris Blue McLain death glare.

Ever since they were kids, Iris had been able to kill with just a look, a look that always made Ivy feel about three feet tall.

Turns out, Iris hadn't lost her touch when it came to her glares.

Ivy shrunk back. "I didn't think so, I just thought I'd ask," she mumbled sheepishly.

Iris just continued to glare, and Ivy continued to feel awful. On second thought, that was a really terrible thing to accuse her sister of doing. Iris knew just as well as anyone how miserable Tiffany and Ezzy had made her life all the way through school. She never would've invited them here on purpose.

Ivy knew that…when she wasn't wrapped up in her own little anger-induced pity party.

When the silence extended out into painful territory, finally Ivy mumbled, "I'm sorry. I shouldn't have said that."

Iris nodded her head – just once, regally, like a queen forgiving her subjects – and just like that, things were okay again. Iris began gathering the potatoes from the kitchen sink and moving them over to the table.

She probably needed to sit down. Ever since her car wreck three months ago, Iris had struggled with simple things, like standing. Or walking. Or staying upright.

It was painful for Ivy to see. Her sister had been the basketball star of Long Valley. She'd helped Sawyer win state championships. She was captain of the girl's basketball team as both a junior *and* a senior. She had more athletic talent in her little pinky toe than Ivy did in her whole body, something the whole valley now knew.

When the high school coach had first welcomed Ivy onto the basketball court, his eyes had been bright with excitement. He'd been handed a gift – another McLain who'd help extend the Sawyer High School winning streak for another three years after Iris had graduated and moved on to college.

It was an excitement that quickly fizzled out when he saw Ivy's ball handling skills, which were…nonexistent.

She'd ended up on the JV team all four years of high school.

That sort of thing just wasn't what a soul could live down in a small town.

Ivy snapped her head up as Iris began to muse, "My best guess is that they heard about the free food and music, and decided to come on down and mooch off us. They're the kinds of people who would think that'd be okay."

Ivy considered that for a moment and then sighed. "You're right." She grabbed the last item – a bowl of washed potatoes – and carried them over to the table for Iris. She should've been paying attention instead of wallowing in her own insecurities, and helped Iris with more of the items. Iris smiled up at her with gratitude anyway, and Ivy forced herself to smile back.

Some days, Iris could be infuriatingly kind. It really wasn't fair that she was *that* pretty and *that* talented and *that* nice.

"Thanks, sis," Iris said cheerfully, oblivious to Ivy's inner turmoil, and drew the bowl towards her, pulling out potatoes so she could begin chopping them.

Ivy headed back to the fruit platter on the counter. Those honeycrisp apples were some of the best she'd ever had, and she couldn't seem to keep her hands off them.

"Well, they've ruined everything," she informed Iris around a mouthful of apple.

"Everything?" Iris echoed skeptically.

"Yeah! There was this guy, and—"

"Hey, you guys, I need to know where you want this table," one of the caterers said, popping his head around the kitchen door.

Iris started to struggle to her feet, but Ivy waved her off. "You sit and take a break and get the damn salad done already. There are rumblings in the ranks that no one has brought the famous McLain salad out yet. I'll go." It was about time she helped out, instead of just mooning over cowboys. She snagged another apple slice and headed out the door, listening as the caterer outlined the issue. She would get this straightened out, and *then* go hide in her parent's broom closet. It was the least she could do for Iris, and for her parents.

It wasn't their fault that returning to Long Valley was the disaster she knew it would be. That blame could be laid squarely at the feet of two women who'd spent years of their lives making Ivy's life miserable…

And one hunky cowboy with *terrible* taste in women.

She was flying back to California tomorrow, and already, she couldn't wait.

CHAPTER 2

AUSTIN

*A*FTER EXTRACTING HIMSELF from Tiffany's loving (read: smothering) embrace, Austin made his way over to Declan's side. Declan was one of the few people at this party who he knew really well, plus there was the fact that he was dating Ivy's sister which made Declan the expert on all things Ivy McLain, at least as far as Austin was concerned.

Once he got to Declan's side, he wracked his brain, trying to think of how to subtly ask for info about Ivy – something a little bit better than "You're banging Ivy's sister and I'd really like to do the same to Ivy" – when Declan's face lit up with laughter. "Damn, Austin, I thought Tiffany was going to strangle you, she was hugging you so hard. How long have you been dating her?"

Austin glared at his best friend. Not many people liked being on the receiving end of laughter, and no surprise, Austin didn't either. "One date. I went on *one date* with her. You'd think I'd proposed to her by the end of it."

Declan let out a shout of laughter that had a couple of nearby people turning their heads to find out what was so funny. Austin did his best to blend into the frozen ground. Attention directed towards him wasn't exactly his favorite thing in the world.

He upped his glaring. Declan laughed louder.

"Man, I can't believe you even went on one date with Tiff. Did she trap you down at the diner?"

"Yes," he groaned, not wanting to admit it out loud. Now that he knew the town better, he'd found out that this was a typical move for Tiffany, but at the time…

He paused, hoping Declan would change

topics, but he was just staring, waiting for more details, so finally Austin mumbled, "It was the first day I was here in Sawyer. I only knew you, and...she was my waitress. Seemed nice. Said we could go to the rodeo together. I thought that sounded like fun, and making a new friend would be nice. I had no idea I was signing up for a lifelong commitment." He scrunched up his face in disgust. "Hell, even Ezzy is possessive, and I didn't even go on a damn date with her!"

Which caused Declan to let out another bark of laughter. "Well," he finally said, wiping the tears from his eyes, "you picked a hell of a girl to become friends with. Tiffany is about as likely to let you go as she is to chip one of her manicured nails doing real work."

Yeah, Austin figured that out − a little too late, but no way to fix that now. "So what's the deal with Ivy?" he asked, as casual as he could manage as they stood side by side, facing towards the groups of people mingling, Christmas music playing quietly through it all.

"I can tell you she's leaving tomorrow," Declan said, serious for the first time. "Ivy hates

Long Valley with a passion, and actually, Tiffany and Ezzy play a big part in that. They made her life a living hell growing up. I tried to defend her a few times from it, but they're girls. I couldn't take 'em out back and punch 'em." He shrugged. "Iris tried to stand up for her too, but…Anyway, Ivy left the night of high school graduation and never looked back. Knowing her, she'll do her best not to be here for another decade, if she can get away with it. Iris practically had to twist her arm off to get her here for this party. She's a California girl, through and through. And the thing is, I'm not sure I blame her."

Austin nodded, soaking the information in. It was too damn bad, really. She sure was cute, what with her dark red hair and easy smile and curves in *all* the right places. It would've been perfect to take her out on a date or two, maybe even wander on over to the diner where Tiffany was a waitress. He could've used her to finally get some breathing room from Tiffany, and Ivy could have gotten her revenge.

But between now and tomorrow? Dammit

all, it wasn't real believable to pretend that he and Ivy had somehow fallen madly in love.

Saying goodbye to Dec, Austin made his way over to the refreshment table to get another cup of mulled apple cider. It was probably a good thing Ivy was leaving, anyway. She was a little too cute and a little too fun to laugh with. He needed to get Tiffany off his back, not find an *actual* girlfriend.

Austin was single, and with any luck, would stay that way for life. He'd tried falling in love once before.

Never again.

CHAPTER 3

IVY

S o WARM. She snuggled down deeper under the covers.

But screaming.

There was screaming.

Why is there screaming?

Ivy jackknifed up in bed. Her mom was screaming and crying, the sound muffled through the closed bedroom door. *Holy hell!* She leaped out of bed and threw on her ratty old bathrobe that she hadn't worn since high school, yanking her bedroom door open, where she promptly plowed *right* into her father, who was also tearing down the hallway.

"Oof!" she grunted.

That made it a second time in two days that she'd run into someone. So much for her waitressing skills keeping her light on her toes.

No time to apologize to her dad or laugh about it, though; they untangled themselves and then were running down the hallway and into the living room, the cries of Betty Rae getting louder as they moved. "Help! Oh God, you have to help! Call 911!"

They rounded the corner into the living room and Ivy skittered to a stop, seeing but not understanding. Her mom was dragging Iris' limp body into the house, covered in blood and melting snow. Iris' eyes were closed; her pale cheeks a stark contrast to the deep red spreading everywhere. Mom laid her down gently and began rocking back and forth over her, crying and stroking her hair away from her face.

"My baby, oh my baby!" she wept, as the blood and the snow swirled together and dripped onto the tile foyer floor.

Ivy just stood there in shock, staring. *How…*

*what...*Her brain refused to comprehend what was in front of her.

Somewhere in the distance, she numbly heard her dad barking into the landline, "My daughter! She fell. She was outside. She hit her head and is bleeding everywhere. Yes...okay... Betty!" he shouted, covering up the mouthpiece of the phone. "The dispatcher wants to know if she's awake or not."

Her mom shook her head. "I've been begging her to wake up, but she isn't movi-innnnggggg..." She broke back down into sobs, rocking back and forth, cradling Iris' head against her. "Iris, baby, wake up for Mom. You have to wake up." The icy winter air curled inside through the open front door, along with snowflakes, still falling endlessly from the sky.

Snow? When did it start snowing? It must've started after her parents' party finished last night. She hated snow. White and cold and endless and...

Ivy's vision blackened around the edges as the world narrowed. She breathed in through her mouth slowly, trying to quell her panic. Iris needed her. Passing out wouldn't help anything. Blood had always been Iris' thing, not Ivy's, and seeing it everywhere, mixed with the hated snow…

The room went a little darker still. Ivy fought it back. She had to. She could help. What would Iris do?

Oh, duh!

She forced herself into the kitchen, where she snatched some hand towels out of the drawer. Iris would stop the bleeding. A ten-year-old kid would know to stop the bleeding. Ivy felt like she was swimming through syrup, everything distorted and moving slow.

Her sister needed her, dammit. She could have a panic attack later. As soon as Iris was okay.

She moved back into the living room, the cold air swirling and mixing with the warm air of the house, but it still wasn't enough and Ivy shivered in her bathrobe, or maybe it was shock settling in. She could be going into shock. She felt shocky. And weird. Her vision was fading in and out with every breath. A distant part of her brain heard the gas heater kick on as she knelt next to Iris, hand towels at the ready.

"Yes, my daughter is putting some towels on her head," Ivy heard her dad tell the dispatcher and with a grimace, she pushed the first towel down. The red of the blood mixed in with the red of Iris' hair, making it deeper and more dramatic against her pale skin, which was growing whiter by the moment. Dammit, she was losing too much blood.

Her mom's tears splashed on Iris' face as she begged God to save her baby. "She's a good girl. She loves everyone. You can't take her away…"

The wail of the ambulance finally made its way into the house and her dad shouted, "Thank you!" to the dispatcher. After a moment, he hung up and rushed over. "Can you feel a pulse?" he demanded.

Her mom nodded. "She's breathing but John, I can't get her to wake up!"

Ivy stared down at her beautiful older sister, red hair encrusted in drying blood, the second kitchen towel starting to soak through so Ivy put a third one on and pushed down, trying to staunch the flow. How could she bleed so much and still be alive?

I'm sorry. I'm so sorry, Iris. I shouldn't have accused you of inviting Tiffany and Ezzy to the party. I should've forced you to move to California with me. There's no snow in San Francisco. You would be okay if you lived there. The shivers only got worse as she stared down at the person she'd always wanted to be. *If you live through this, I promise to help you move to California. I'll take care of you there. You've always taken care of me; it's time for me to take care of you. Please wake up. I need to tell you how sorry I am.*

The wails were incredibly loud and then hurrying feet crunched through the hated white snow, still swirling from the sky, and then they were in the house. The EMT eased Ivy's grasp from the bloodied towels and with practiced efficiency, the two EMTs loaded her up onto a stretcher, pushing her outside and into the back of the ambulance.

Ivy stared after them through the open door, frozen to the floor, as her mom and dad begged the emergency personnel for more information.

"We're taking her to the Long Valley Hospital. The Life Flight helicopter is on its way and should be landing shortly. We aren't equipped to take care of this kind of brain injury here, especially with the previous trauma she's had. We'll fly her to St Luke's in Boise from there. There isn't enough room in the helicopter for any passengers, so you'll need to drive and meet up with her there."

Ivy forced herself to her feet, stiff and so very cold. She wasn't sure if it was from kneeling just inside an open door, letting in the arctic air, or the terror from seeing her sister hurt. She made herself throw the towels away in the kitchen trash, and then scrub her hands clean of the dark and crusty blood. She had to clean up. She had to get dressed. She would go with her parents to Boise, and she would take care of her sister.

Her parents were coming back in, shouting as they hurried to get dressed, and as Ivy slipped a sweatshirt over her head, she suddenly realized that today was the day she was supposed to be going back to California. Her mom was supposed to be driving her to Boise this morning, but not to see her comatose sister in the hospital, but so she could fly back home.

Panic clutched at her again. There was no way she could leave Iris. Not now. Not when her sister needed her. When Iris had originally gotten into her car wreck just over three months ago, Ivy hadn't been able to afford to fly up to see her, and had been forced to sit on the sidelines as her sister made her slow recovery.

Ivy couldn't do it again.

Screw her job. Screw her boss. He was going to be angry when he heard the news, but she couldn't find it in herself to care.

Iris needed her, and this time, Ivy wasn't going to let her down.

CHAPTER 4

AUSTIN

THE CLEAR, BITTERLY COLD AIR hurt his lungs with every breath, with a cloud drifting up from the nostrils of Bob as they plodded along. It was the perfect winter day – cold, bright, and beautiful, ice and snow sparkling as far as the eye could see.

He'd thought about asking Declan to go riding with him this morning, but then decided against it, figuring he was probably spending all of his free time with Iris. After being apart for years, Austin knew it only made sense that his friend would want to spend as much time as possible with her, although it did leave Austin wanting for companionship of his own.

Too bad Ivy has gone back to California.

Austin shoved that thought away. Ivy was gone, and wouldn't be back. One moment of staring at each other, almost kissing, before that damn Tiffany showed up, did *not* a relationship make.

Which was fine. Good, even. He didn't want a relationship. He apparently just had to remind himself of this fact more often in the last four days than he normally had to, was all.

He saw a glint of red through the trees, and sat up straighter in the saddle. He must be losing it. He'd spent so much time forcing himself not to think about Ivy McLain that he'd begun to see her out in the wilds of Idaho.

Bob stepped through the snow, carefully setting down each hoof to make it through the treacherous footing, while Austin kept his eyes trained on the dark red blob of color, growing larger by the moment.

That's…

That's really her!

He'd recognize that brilliant red hair anywhere, falling in curly waves over a dark blue jacket. The same dark blue jacket Ivy had been wearing the other night at the party.

He broke into the small clearing to see her perched on a rock, a notepad spread open on her lap as she sketched, staring down at the pad and then up again into the distance. He squinted, trying to figure out what it was she was drawing, when she heard the jingle of Bob's bridle and turned with a squeal, snapping the notepad shut.

"Oh!" she exclaimed, her hand over her chest, staring at him like he'd just descended from an alien spacecraft. He smiled, trying to put her at ease.

"Hey," he said, swinging down from his horse, patting his dark brown coat on the side for a moment before turning back to Ivy. "What are you doing here?"

The words came out before he could think through them, a rarity in his world. He usually thought through every word, every statement, before he even opened his mouth, but somehow, around Ivy, things just came out.

Sometimes, horribly awkward things, implying shit he didn't mean.

Her eyebrows snapped together in a glower. "I've always come here, way before *you* moved to town," she told him pertly. "I've been coming here for years. What are *you* doing here?"

He rubbed the back of his neck, wishing he could start this conversation over again. Finding her in his favorite thinking spot had rattled him. He needed to get this conversation back on track. "I found it when I first moved here. I like it. The creek is nice during the summer, although it's frozen solid right now, of course, and the view of the Goldfork Mountains..." He pointed to them, as if she wouldn't know where in the hell the Goldfork Mountains were, and then rolled his eyes at himself. Ivy grew up in Long Valley. She knew the area better than he did. He did *not* need to give her a geography lesson.

He wasn't exactly doing a good job of getting the conversation back on track, something her deepening glower was only reinforcing.

"What are you still doing in Long Valley?" he tried again. "Declan said you were going to leave the day after the party."

Okay, so that made it worse.

Much worse. In a totally-different-way worse, but that wasn't exactly a consolation at that moment.

Ivy stood up, tucking her notepad under her arm, and then walked over to Bob, letting him snuffle her hand before she began stroking his long neck. She shot Austin a knowing grin as she petted Bob, letting the silence stretch out between them, obviously picking up on the implication that Austin had been asking Declan about her, and reveling in it.

Dammit! That was *not* what he'd wanted to tell her. It was stalkerish and weird, and he didn't want her to know that he'd been that interested after their literal run-in with each other.

He fished around for something to say, someway to get himself out of this pickle without making it even worse, something he seemed completely incapable of today, when she finally took pity on him. "I wish I could say it was a good thing that I'm still here." She paused, her breath disappearing in a cloud around her head, her smile fading. "Iris is going to be at St. Luke's for at least another week, though."

They were close enough now for him to see the dark flecks in her otherwise brilliant blue eyes, and the dark bags under her eyes. He wouldn't exactly consider himself to be an expert on Ivy, but even he could see that she looked exhausted.

"I'm so sorry," he said quietly. "I hadn't heard."

"The gossip chain here in Long Valley must really be broken then," Ivy said with a small laugh. "Usually, this kind of thing gets around town, *almost* before it happens. Somehow, Sawyer is constantly breaking the time-space continuum, and yet, no scientists have shown up to study this phenomenon."

They both laughed for just a moment at that, and then quickly sobered up. It almost felt irreverent to laugh under the circumstances.

"So what happened to Iris? Did she get into another car wreck?" He hadn't met her before the wreck, of course, although while he and Declan were college roommates up at the University of Idaho, he'd sure heard a lot about her. When they'd first met after Iris moved back to town, Austin had looked her over discretely, searching for her angel wings. Declan had made her seem one step short of perfection, and although Austin had thought her plenty nice, she wasn't…

Well, she wasn't Ivy, that was for sure. Something about Ivy made his heart skip a beat in his chest, an altogether unexpected and not entirely desired reaction.

"No, no car wreck, thank God. Although the whole thing happened because of that." Bob whinnied and nudged Ivy's hand, obviously growing discontented at the amount of attention he was getting from her, which made Austin roll his eyes inwardly. Bob always was a glutton for love. Unlike other horses that could take it or leave it, Bob lived for it. Ivy absentmindedly began stroking him again, her eyes focused off in the distance. "Mom found her outside. Iris had thought she ought to clean off her own front steps after that snowstorm the night of my parent's party. I swear, her stubbornness is going to get her killed."

She focused back on him, a small smile on her lips. "We McLains excel at a lot of things, but stubbornness is truly our crowning achievement."

A bark of laughter tore out of him at that. He guessed it was a real good thing that Iris had hooked up with Declan, then, because he had never met someone more stubborn than Declan. Not even his parents, and that was saying something.

"So when are you heading back to California?" he asked, and she cocked an eyebrow at him. He cursed inwardly again. She hadn't told him she lived in California; they hadn't had enough time to get that far during their one and only encounter.

"You spy a lot on girls you meet at anniversary parties?" she asked dryly, but then spared him from coming up with a suitable response.

Which was good, because he had none. "I'll be here another couple of days. I hadn't planned on that originally, something that you seem to already know—"

He coughed, his cheeks turning red.

The cold was getting to him. That was it. He did *not* blush, so no other explanation made sense.

"—but since I've been here this long, why not stay a little longer, you know? I want to make sure Iris is okay before I head back home."

Austin nodded, his mind going a million miles a minute. If she was staying on a little longer, well…

"While you're here in town, want to go out sometime?" As soon as the words left his mouth, he felt like an idiot. She probably had a boyfriend back in California. As beautiful as she was, she probably had *ten* boyfriends back in California. She wouldn't want to hang out with him.

And yet, she didn't laugh him off, or ridicule the idea. She didn't even gently let him down. Instead, she just cocked her head to the side and said contemplatively, "And if I said yes, where would you take me?"

Oh shit.

Since he hadn't exactly planned on asking her out, he most certainly didn't have a specific place in mind. "Somewhere" wasn't going to work as an answer. He scrambled, trying to come up with something.

"The bells concert!" he said triumphantly, thrilled that his brain had come up with something better than, "Ummmm…" which was originally all that it was supplying him with. "The annual bells concert at the Methodist Church. I didn't get to go the last couple of years, and I'd love to have someone to attend with me."

The truth was, it was awkward as hell to go out to public events like concerts by himself, and going with Declan would seem too much like they were dating, which would send all sorts of wrong signals to this tiny mountain town. So, he'd stayed away from pretty much every public event in Long Valley since he'd moved there, despite the fact that this left him lonely most nights.

Which he liked. Of course. He didn't want to find a girlfriend. He was happy being alone.

Somehow, the idea of going to the bells concert with Ivy made him even happier, though.

She stood there for a long while, staring at him, her eyes inscrutable, until she finally nodded. "Okay," she said softly.

"Okay," he repeated, half stunned. He'd somehow expected her to say no, and he couldn't shake the feeling that she was almost as surprised by her answer as he was.

He wasn't one to look a gift horse in the mouth, though, so he swung up on Bob to ride away before she could change her mind. "See you at 6:30 at your parent's house?" When she nodded her assent, he wheeled Bob around and headed back out of the clearing, a tuneless whistle echoing through the snowy forest as he made his way back to the trailhead.

Today was turning out to be a pretty damn good day.

CHAPTER 5

IVY

TODAY WAS TURNING OUT to be a *horrible* day. Ivy paced the confines of her childhood bedroom, feeling the walls closing in on her.

First, she'd been drawing the Goldfork Mountains, and she just didn't do that kind of thing. She'd made it a point years ago not to draw landscapes, and certainly not to draw *Idaho* landscapes. She was a California girl, dammit, and did her best to pretend she'd never even heard of Idaho most days.

But then, on top of that slip-up, she'd said

yes to Austin's offer to go to the bells concert, a concert she'd spent most of her teenage years doing her best to avoid.

The last time she'd gone was in the 9th grade. Tiffany and Ezzy had sat behind her and had pulled her hair anytime they thought no one was looking. She'd turned around and glared at them, but they'd simply send her angelic stares, shrugging their shoulders dramatically. She hadn't wanted to whine to her parents – what kind of a baby whined to their parents about someone pulling their hair – so she'd suffered through the concert quietly.

She always mysteriously had a headache the night of the bells concert after that.

Going back there was…

She shivered, feeling a little ill at the thought. That night had been the start of the bullying – Tiffany and Ezzy had never been best buds with her, and they'd teased her a few times previously, but that night was when it really began, and didn't stop until she walked off the auditorium stage the night of graduation and never looked back.

They were, in a roundabout way, the reason why she was in the predicament she was in. If she hadn't pushed herself to be successful, or at least appear to—

She heard thumping up in the attic, side-tracking her from her thoughts. Was her dad cleaning the attic? She smiled sadly to herself. That was so like her dad – keeping himself busy while waiting for something useful to do. He wasn't one to sit around, waiting for the world to come to him.

If he couldn't fix Iris and make her all better, well dammit, he'd clean out the attic.

She wandered out into the hallway, working her way around the fold-down ladder, extending from the ceiling. She could see dust motes dancing in the air of the attic. Truthfully, it was probably a disaster up there, and deserved to be cleaned, whether or not Iris was in the hospital.

"Iv—! Oh hi, there you are," he said, spotting her as he peered down through the opening. "Look at what I found." He extended out a dusty plastic container to her, and she climbed up onto the lowest rung of the ladder so she could grab it. "Your art supplies from high school," he proudly announced, as if she couldn't already tell what it was she was holding.

"Thanks, Dad," she said, feeling a little choked up at the sight. She cleared her throat. She looked up at him, peering down through the attic door opening, cobwebs stuck in his hair and spread across his shirt, giving him the appearance of having lived in – or at least decorated – a haunted house. She smiled a little. "Hey, do you think it'd be okay if I went back to Boise tomorrow?"

When Iris had first woken up in the hospital, she'd been frantic with worry about not telling Declan she was there. She'd become so agitated, the head nurse had told the McLains that they were only allowed to have one visitor in the room at a time, so they'd have to decide among them who that'd be.

Mom had won that prize, of course, and hadn't left Iris' side since then. Dad and Ivy had driven back to Sawyer to wait the doctors out. It had been four days – surely they'd allow someone else in there by now.

"Yeah, the doctor has said that we can start having two visitors starting tomorrow. After I find Iris' teddy bear, I was going to drive over there and spell your momma so she could come back home and sleep in a real bed tonight. Tomorrow, though, I know she'll want to come back. You could hitch a ride with her then."

Ivy had to hide her laugh at the thought of Iris getting her teddy bear from childhood delivered to her at the hospital. It was sweet of her dad to think of it, although Iris, at age 35, was a little old for stuffed animals.

It made her dad feel useful, though, and that was what mattered.

"Thanks for the supplies, Dad. Oh, and I'm going to be going to the bells concert tonight over at the Methodist Church." She tried to slip it in there casually, as if it was no big deal, but of course, her dad wasn't fooled in the slightest.

"Are you going with someone in particular?"

She shifted the heavy box to her other hip, trying to ignore the fact that she was 32 years old and having to report her dating activities to her father.

This is why she could never move back in with her parents, no matter how poor she became.

Also, why did she have to have this conversation while her father was hanging out above her in the ceiling? Her neck was really starting to cramp up. She rolled it side to side as she mumbled, "Austin Bishop." She looked back up at her dad. "He was at the party. You've met him?"

"Oh, the new extension agent? He took over after Mr. Snow retired. Nice kid."

Ivy did roll her eyes at that. Austin looked about her age, although she hadn't actually quizzed him on the topic, but regardless, he was a little old to be referred to as a "kid." But, her dad would always consider someone her age to be a child, no matter what.

Something she was well aware of.

"Well anyway, he invited me and I thought it'd be fun to go. Something to do to keep my mind off…things," she ended vaguely, but her dad knew what she meant.

That comment didn't need any clarification. Not right now.

He nodded. "Does this mean that you're not going to be struck by a sudden headache right before the concert?"

She gaped up at him in surprise. "Dad!" she choked out through her laughter and he just grinned down at her and shrugged.

"Just because I'm your dad doesn't mean I'm completely unobservant, despite what your teenage soul probably thought. Was it those two girls?"

Ivy's breath caught and she just stared at him, the laughter gone. He'd known? She'd tried so hard to hide all of that from her parents. Pride had demanded that she had. "Yeah," she said softly.

"I never knew what to do about them," he admitted. "I wish I could've…" His voice trailed off into nothingness, and then he harrumphed his way back onto stable ground. Discussing feelings was never her father's strong suit. "Well anyway, I need to find that teddy bear so I can drive to Boise before it gets too dark outside." He disappeared from view, heading back into the depths of the attic.

Ivy clutched the art supplies box to her chest, feeling a small smile spread across her face. Not having any access to art, except paper and pencil, had been one of the tougher parts about this visit to Idaho, and that was saying something. She hadn't expected to be gone this long, or she would've figured out how to pack the supplies in, even if it'd meant leaving a pair of shoes behind or something.

But now…

She headed back into her bedroom and dropped the box on the bed, where she unsnapped the lockdown handles and pulled the lid off to stare down in wonderment. She'd been such a snob as a kid. She'd been so sure that she'd have amazing, top-quality art supplies when she went off to college, and as such, hadn't packed any of her high school art supplies. She hadn't wanted to taint her future by using inferior products.

After paying rent and tuition and books, though, she'd quickly abandoned her lofty (read: snotty) dreams and went right back to using the same brands she always had. She'd learned that she didn't need $50 paintbrushes to make a beautiful art piece.

She pulled the items out one by one – the oils, the trays, the brushes, even a small unused canvas – and grinned to herself. She needed to do something while in Long Valley to keep herself sane. Other than go on pointless dates with handsome cowboys, of course.

Hold on…

Her hands froze over a well-worn eraser.

Why is Austin asking me out on a date?

Somehow, among everything else, Ivy hadn't thought this through, but duh – Austin already had a girlfriend. Tiffany had made that very, very clear the night of her parent's party. Although the irony of Austin cheating on Tiffany with Ivy would be rich indeed, Ivy wasn't willing to be the third part of that triangle.

Let Austin cheat on his girlfriend with some other unsuspecting soul. Ivy McLain wasn't going to have anything to do with it.

She felt the anger build up in her. Cheating,

lying asshole. He *deserved* Tiffany. The pair would make each other very, very happy.

She grabbed her cell phone, ready to dash off an angry text message, telling Austin that he could stuff this date where the sun didn't shine, when she stopped, staring at her phone in frustration. Not only had she failed to realize that she was about to help Austin become a cheater, she'd also failed to get his number.

Which meant she'd just have to wait to tell him off in person. Well good. And while she was at it, she could inform him of her thoughts about his taste in women. Which, aside from wanting to go on a date with her of course, was downright atrocious.

"Hey Iv, I'm heading out," her dad said at her bedroom door, holding up Iris' beloved teddy bear as evidence of his success. "I'll see you tomorrow — have fun at the concert, eh?"

She nodded, forcing a smile onto her face. Her dad had enough to worry about. He didn't need to worry about the fact that his daughter was going to miss yet another bells concert for yet another awful reason. His footsteps faded as he headed out.

Ivy turned to face her bed again, and all of her art supplies. It was time to keep herself occupied. Too busy to think was exactly what she needed right now. She could face reality later.

CHAPTER 6

AUSTIN

AUSTIN PULLED UP in front of the McLain house, his stomach strangely rumbly and unsettled. It wasn't exactly happy about this state of affairs, and he stared down at it for a moment, unsure of what to attribute this case of nerves to. He was going on a date with Ivy to get Tiffany off his back. Ivy could exact revenge on Tiffany by going out with the one guy Tiffany had been gunning after for months. All would be well with the world.

Feelings, or stomach linings for that matter, need not be involved.

He jumped out of his truck and crunched

through the snow, a few lackadaisical flakes still drifting down from the sky. The passing storm gave off the impression that it couldn't be bothered to put on a real show, something that he wasn't sure he blamed it for. It was *cold*. It was hard to do anything with much enthusiasm.

He knocked on the door and then stood back, an expectant smile on his face. At least going to the Methodist Church could be done with great enthusiasm. He'd always loved Christmas music, so a whole concert, played by bells, dedicated to holiday tunes…it didn't get much better than that. He was right on time, and if they left right away, he figured they'd be able to get great seats. It was going to be a fun ni—

"You!" Ivy shouted angrily, even before she got the front door completely open. He stared at her, wide-eyed. She had paint streaked across her nose, a bit in her hair, and seemed to be in the process of spreading it around even more liberally as she shook her paintbrush at him. "How dare you!"

She slammed the door in his face. He stared

at it. She yanked it open. "I'm not letting you off that easy!" she announced angrily. "Get in here so I can yell at you proper, without letting all the warm air out."

He debated for a moment – he could just make a run for the truck. An irate Ivy wasn't exactly a fun sight to behold, especially when that anger was directed at him, but he finally decided that the curiosity about why she was so angry would drive him crazy. He had to know.

Then he'd make a run for the truck and never come back.

Poor Declan. These McLain girls look sweet on the surface, but…

He sidled past her and her wildly arcing paintbrush, and into the house. She slammed the door and rounded on him, shaking the brush with every step as she advanced towards him.

"You asshole!" she said, her face roughly the same color as her hair. "You would take me out to the concert when you already have a girlfriend? I can't believe you. Did you think that just because I'm from San Francisco, it's okay to take me out for a night on the town and just hope that your girlfriend never hears about it? Well, even if you have *atrocious* taste in women, that's on you, not me. I'm not going to help you be a cheater, Mr. I'm-Just-An-Aww-Shucks Cowboy. I'm not fooled by that...that...*face!*" She jabbed the paintbrush at him, almost whacking said face, and he darted out of range at just the last moment.

They stared at each other, her breathing heavily as she glowered, and then...he couldn't help it. He busted up laughing.

"What are you laughing about?" she demanded, jamming her hands down onto her hips.

He wiped the tears from his eyes. "You. The paintbrush." He doubled over laughing again. He could see her tapping her foot on the floor out of the corner of his eye, *obviously* not impressed by his reaction. He took a few deep breaths and straightened up. She was angry, and he wasn't helping matters by laughing. Although he imagined he'd remember the sight of Ivy swinging a paint brush around in the air, jabbing it like a rapier, for the rest of his life.

"I'm guessing you're talking about Tiffany?" he asked, once he'd managed to become serious again.

She nodded, just once, glaring at him through narrowed eyes. He held his hands up beseechingly.

"So I know what Tiffany made it seem like," he said slowly, quietly. "The night of the party, right?" Ivy nodded again. "She and I are not a *thing*, no matter what she may think or hope for. We've gone on one date, and I haven't been able to get rid of her since. I'm sorry she made you believe that I would be a cheater, but I promise, there's nothing between us."

She stared at him, consideringly for a moment, and then inspiration struck. He grinned in triumph. "Hey, you like Declan, right?"

"Sometimes. Sometimes, he's just an ass who left my sister fifteen years ago without explanation and broke her heart, something *I* had to help her get over."

Oh. That didn't exactly go how he'd expected it to. Telling her that Declan would never be best friends with an asshole was not going to help his case.

Time to change tactics.

"Listen, I'm from up north – Coeur d'Alene, up in the panhandle. I moved here to become the extension agent, and I only knew Declan when I rolled into town. We'd been roommates for a year up at the U of I, and he was the one to suggest that I apply for the extension agent position when Mr. Snow retired.

"Anyway, the first day I was in town, I met Tiffany down at the diner. She was my waitress. She asked me to hang out with her at the rodeo, I agreed, and she's been clinging tighter to me than ivy growing up a brick wall ever since." He studied her face for a moment, which was open and listening, but she hadn't made a decision. Not yet.

He drew in a deep breath. *Here goes nothing.* He hadn't planned on bringing this up with Ivy, since it was hard to know how a girl would take news like this, but he only had one card left to play. It was time to play it and hope for the best. "Truthfully, I was thinking you might be up for helping me out with this. Declan mentioned that Tiffany and you didn't exactly get along in high school."

Ivy's pinched face at that comment told him all he needed to know. "So," he continued urgently, "if you go to the concert with me, she's *really* going to be upset. I figure, it's great revenge, right?"

Ivy continued to study his face for a moment, and then a small smile broke out on her face, which quickly spread into a huge grin. "That, sir, is a terrific idea. I like how you think!" She laughed, leaning forward and popping a quick kiss on his cheek. "I need to go get changed and ready. I'll be right back."

She disappeared up the hallway to what he assumed was her bedroom. He stared down the dark corridor, rubbing his cheek idly, the skin burning where her lips had touched.

Well, he was right about one thing: A date with Ivy definitely wasn't going to be boring.

She soon reappeared, paint scrubbed clean from her face, clean clothes instead of paint-spattered ones. She'd put on a loose sweater that draped across her body, belted into place just below a very generous chest, with stretchy jeans disappearing into knee-high boots. He wished for a moment that he could get a better view of her ass, but decided, as he watched her swaying hips from behind as they headed to his truck, that it was probably for the best that he couldn't. He needed to be decent for this trip to a church, no matter what his brain wanted.

They made their way to his diesel truck that he'd left running while inside. It was too cold to turn his truck on and off, plus he'd need it to stay warm long enough to get through the concert without freezing up. Just this quick jaunt from the front door to the truck had bitter cold seeping into his bones, and he heard a happy sigh of relief from her as he helped Ivy up into the warmth of the truck. Her dark blue jacket looked pretty thin, and she didn't seem to own gloves, or at least wasn't disposed to wearing them. It was too damn cold outside to not wear gloves, in his humble opinion.

Girls were so weird sometimes.

He kept that thought to himself; instead just

heading towards the church that was only a couple of blocks away. Even before they pulled into the parking lot, he could hear the Christmas music spilling out of it, the warm light and stained glass windows drawing distorted, gorgeous designs on the ground. He pulled into a parking spot and cut the engine, the sudden silence after the loud rumble feeling almost deafening. "You ready?" he asked her.

She was wringing her hands together, looking as if she were debating between bolting for home or throwing up, but she nodded. Somewhere between home and here, she'd had time to think about their plan, and realized that it meant seeing Tiffany, which probably wasn't her favorite activity in the world. Before he could offer to take her back home, though, she responded.

"I'm ready," she said. Her voice wasn't exactly steady, but he decided not to mention how unconvincing she sounded, and instead just helped her out of the truck. Once her feet were on the snowy ground, she looked up at him, her soft blue eyes large enough to drown in, and he grinned down at her, trying to project his confidence onto her.

"Let's give 'em a show," he said softly in her ear, and then tucked her hand into his arm as they strolled towards the doors of the church. He felt her arm tremble in his, so he tucked it closer against his side.

He wondered if she'd fought him so hard on going to the concert because not-so-deep-down inside, she really didn't want to go. Ivy had worked hard to wipe her feet clean of this town, and never come back. He'd asked her out because she was cute and fun and he hadn't been able to stop thinking about her for four days and he needed some way of getting Tiffany off his back, but at no point had he thought about what *she* wanted or needed, which pretty much made him a Class A asshole.

He needed to apologize, but maybe not in the midst of a community concert. He'd apologize afterwards, while driving her home.

To be willing to face a town that had made her life miserable for years on end...

Despite her trembling, or maybe because of

it, Austin couldn't help but be impressed by her backbone. She was damn brave, whether or not she realized it.

They walked up the front steps and into the foyer of the church, the welcoming warmth of the building enveloping them like a fleece blanket next to a roaring fire. Her trembling only increased, though.

"We can go home," he whispered into her ear, wanting to give her one last chance to make a run for the door. He couldn't help but draw in her smell as he leaned close, letting it wash over him. Cinnamon and chocolate – she smelled like the best kind of dessert. How did she make her hair smell like *chocolate*?

Before he could blurt out that question though, which would've been horrifying, she responded, saving him from complete embarrassment. "I'm fine," she whispered back. "Just don't let go of my arm."

That was something he was happy to oblige her on, and hugged it tighter against his side.

The concert was non-denominational – simply a community event that happened to be held in the Methodist Church – and so no pastor greeted them upon their entrance, although Austin saw a few farmers from around the valley that he'd worked with over the past two years in the audience. His gaze swept the chapel, looking for Tiffany or Ezzy, and finally he blew out a breath at the same time that Ivy relaxed.

They weren't there. That meant that the purpose of the date was moot, of course – they could just turn around and go home.

But…he didn't want to. He wanted to enjoy an evening out on the town with a beautiful woman, whether or not that date had a hidden reason for happening.

So instead of heading for the front doors like they really should have, he guided her towards a mostly empty bench where she settled against his side as he casually draped his arm across the back of the bench. They fit together, her soft curves melding against his side.

He wasn't quite sure what to think about that. None of this was what he'd planned, and yet…it felt right.

Before he could ponder *that* thought further,

the music piping through the speakers dropped off, and a conductor strode up onto the front dais to the podium. After welcoming them out to the 57th Long Valley Bells Concert, the musicians began filing in from either side of the church, and up to rows of tables already marching in lines across the front of the chapel. Huge bells as big as watermelons down to tiny bells the size of his thumb all gleamed in the Christmas twinkle lights and candles occupying every space possible.

As the chandeliers above dimmed, leaving the twinkling lights and flickering candles to provide most of the light, the musicians started out with a rousing rendition of *Carol of the Bells*, the notes echoing from the arched ceiling, swirling and surrounding them with the gorgeous sound. Ivy turned and grinned up at him, joy rolling off her in waves, and he snuggled her closer to his side. The fun of the moment was contagious, and he couldn't help but revel in it.

Even though absolutely none of this evening was going to plan, Austin found himself on his feet, clapping enthusiastically as the musicians took bow after bow at the end of the concert. He couldn't contain the grin that seemed permanently attached to his face. He looked down at Ivy, who was grinning back just as widely, and felt his heart thump a little harder than normal.

That felt…weird. All tingly and shit.

He put his arm around her and guided her towards the foyer of the church, joining the stream of people headed the same direction. He decided that he needed to watch what he ate for lunch. Those jalapeños were causing heartburn. He felt a little young to need to watch his diet, but obviously *something* had gone wrong between his fajitas at lunch and now.

Because it couldn't be anything more than that.

CHAPTER 7

IVY

Ivy's waist tingled where it was pressed up against Austin, as they followed the flow of the crowd back into the foyer. The bells choir had put out refreshments — coffee, hot cocoa, apple cider, and some homemade donuts — and following her nose, Ivy decided to head that direction instead of out the front doors. Those donuts looked *way* too delicious to pass up.

After she and Austin picked out cups of coffee and donuts, though, she quickly realized her mistake. More than a few members of the community were openly eyeing them, and the same question was written on every person's face – was Ivy dating Austin? Had Ivy moved back to Long Valley? Had Ivy given up on her dream of becoming a famous artist and had slunk back home with her tail stuck between her legs?

She felt the burning desire to pull a chair over from the corner, stand on it, clear her throat, and announce to the world that she and Austin were *not* dating; they were simply attending the same concert in close proximity to each other.

Unless the story was being retold to Tiffany and Ezzy, in which case Austin was madly in love with her.

She thought back to leaning against his side as the music had swirled around them, his rock-hard muscular abs the perfect balance to her flabby, fat self, and decided that perhaps making such an announcement wouldn't be a grand idea, mostly because she wasn't sure she could make it sound convincing.

She'd enjoyed leaning against his side, dammit. She'd enjoyed having his arm around her shoulders as they'd sat there. It made her sound like she was in junior high all over again — excited about nothing but snuggling with a boy — but she couldn't seem to help it.

He looked down at her, obviously noticing the same number of stares that she had, and said, "Ready to head out?" in a jovial-if-overly-loud tone of voice. He was trying to save her from embarrassment, which was…sweet.

Really sweet.

Unfortunately, he'd caught her mid-bite into the donut, jelly oozing out the sides, and so she couldn't do anything more than just nod her agreement.

She really should stop eating jelly donuts. They were just so damn *good*.

A couple of older farmers in the area said their goodbyes to Austin on the way out of the church, but no one said anything to her. Hell, they might not have even recognized her. It'd been years since she'd been back in Long Valley.

Ugh. Who was she kidding? She was Ivy McLain, one of the two McLain girls in town, and her brilliant red hair, even more vibrant in color than Iris', was not exactly easy to miss.

Ivy licked her fingers clean as they made their way back to the truck, trying to get the sticky sugary wonder that was Mrs. Frank's Homemade Donuts off her fingers, when she heard Austin clearing his throat. She looked up at him and caught a strangled look of panic? Lust? flitting across his face before it was replaced by a smile. It was so fast, she wasn't sure if she'd even seen it, or if she'd just imagined it. She studied his face for a moment longer and then decided that since the lighting wasn't so great in the oversized parking lot, she was probably just seeing things.

After he helped her into the truck, he hurried around to his side, but instead of heading home, he started driving the streets of Sawyer.

"I thought you'd want to get out of there," he said as way of explanation, as he turned down another street bedecked with Christmas lights. There went the house of her sixth grade crush. Oh, and there was her high school debate teacher's house.

It was so weird being back in Long Valley. Every street was filled to the brim with…memories. She wasn't sure if this was a good thing or bad, although she was heavily leaning in the direction of bad.

Memories of Long Valley were pretty much never good.

She realized she'd been silent too long. "Yeah," she said quickly, trying to fill in the hole created by her wandering mind. "I haven't been home in a while, so I'm sure a couple of people were wondering what I was doing there." *Not only that, but what I was doing there with* you.

She kept that thought to herself. If Austin hadn't yet noticed that she wasn't the most gorgeous girl in town, she wasn't about to inform him of the need for glasses.

"So what do you do in California?" Austin asked.

Ivy felt a bit of panic lodge itself in her throat. *Wait tables while pretending to be a successful artist.* Somehow, she was pretty sure that wasn't a great answer, so she swallowed it whole. "I went to the California College of the Arts, where I got my Bachelors of Fine Arts degree in Painting and Drawing," she said with an overly cheerful grin. "Iris was always the one with the athletic talent, while I was the artistic one. Iris is lucky if she can pull off a stick-figure drawing, which is only fair. I have to beat her at *something*, right?"

At the genuine chuckle from Austin, Ivy felt her stomach unclench just a smidge. She'd spent her entire life trying to live up to Iris' example, and had failed on every count. Not as tall, not as pretty, not as skinny, not as athletic, not as well loved by every person who met her…

Compared to her ultra-perfect sister, Ivy was pretty much a failure. Except when it came to art. It was a world where she'd always excelled.

Until she actually had to pay her rent with her work, at which point she was once again a failure.

She pushed that thought away. No reason to focus on that. Not tonight.

"When did you decide that you wanted to be an artist?" Austin asked as they turned down yet another wintry street. This one had a home where they'd gone all out, complete with a Nativity Scene made of blow-up dolls. Ivy bit back her grin at the sight. Somehow, Baby Jesus being represented by a blob of inflated plastic just didn't fit her idea of the Christmas season, but she obviously had different views than the owner of 437 Oak Street.

"The first time I won a coloring contest. The Shop 'N Go holds one every year, and I won my division when I was a kindergartener. I won my division every year until I graduated from high school. It started out with a prize for a candy bar of my choice, and worked its way up until I got a $250 scholarship when I was a senior in high school. At the time, I really thought $250 was a ton of money and was going to get me somewhere. It wasn't until I got to San Francisco and enrolled in my classes that I realized that it only barely covered one textbook."

Austin looked at her and grinned. "I'm happy to hear that colleges are just as expensive in California as they are in North Idaho," he said dryly. "I'd hate to hear I overpaid for my secondary education."

They laughed together, the happiness rushing through her chest as she grinned back at him. Ever since high school, she'd hated cowboys. They were assholes who broke her heart and made fun of her to other students. They were also dumb hicks who couldn't count unless they removed their boots and socks first.

But talking to Austin…he was this totally different creature from every other cowboy she'd ever met. He didn't chew tobacco or say "ain't" or…

Kiss girls under bleachers while his girlfriend stupidly waited for him to come sit next to her to watch a football game.

Her eyes searched his face. Well, maybe he did. Maybe he did all of those things, and she just hadn't seen that side of him yet. It wasn't like she'd spent years in his company or something. She was being awfully naïve, simply believing that he was a good guy who wouldn't pull that kind of stunt because she *wanted* it to be true.

What kind of proof did she have to back that belief up? The fact that he was adorable when he smiled?

That wasn't proof. That was her hormones talking.

That was nothing but wishful thinking.

"So what kind of artwork do you do?" he asked, breaking into her thoughts. "Paint? Sculpt? Draw?"

"Oil paints," she said, "although I always sketch out what I'm going to do beforehand. I tend to paint abstract expressionism, which is all the rage down in Cali right now."

And then he was asking her questions and she was answering, and she realized how much fun it was to talk about art with a novice, who didn't have any preconceived notions about what was the *best* kind of art, or the most *sophisticated* kind of art. It was such a different way of looking at art from what she was used to, what between her art teachers at college and the art gallery owners she'd finally managed to make friends with, all of whom were focused on the latest trends, the biggest names.

Austin had an earthy way of looking at art that was...unpretentious. She started laughing at one point. "I bet you think that antlers are a perfectly valid decorating style, don't you?" she asked in a half-accusatory tone of voice.

He grinned over at her. "Have you been peeking in my living room window while I was sleeping?" he demanded. "There's a four-point right over my couch that all the guys down at Frank's Feed are jealous of."

She bust out laughing. "I bet they are…"

He pulled to a stop and Ivy blinked, realizing that he'd finally made his way to her home when she hadn't been paying attention. He hurried around to the passenger side of the truck and helped her down, tucking her arm in his as they made their way to the dark front door. She shoved her other hand into her pocket, wishing for the hundredth time that she'd thought to bring her gloves with her from California. Not that they would be a lot of use in this weather, since they were more for show than function, but they would have to do *some* good in this sub-zero weather she'd inexplicably found herself in.

They reached the front steps, lit only by a string of Christmas lights marching across the roofline of the house, and Ivy paused. Was he going to kiss her? Hug her? Tell her have a good life and drive off into the night?

He pulled her against him and hugged her tight. "Goodnight, Ivy," he said softly into her hair. "Thanks for hanging out with me tonight."

And then he was gone, crunching his way back to his truck, and she was left alone on her parents' front doorstep, staring after him, uncertain if she was happy or sad that he hadn't taken a chance and kissed her.

It was probably for the best, but a part of her still wished for something more.

CHAPTER 8

AUSTIN

*H*E CLIMBED INTO HIS TRUCK and settled back against his leather seat, staring out into the darkness, cut through by his headlights. Small flakes continued to drift down through the beams of light trying so valiantly to penetrate the darkness.

"Austin Bishop, you're an idiot," he said out loud. When he'd seen her lick her fingers clean of the sugar and jam from the donuts, he wasn't sure if he'd ever breathe again. It had to be the most innocently erotic thing he'd ever seen in his life. He'd wanted to drive her around after that, if only to calm his libido down before dropping her off at home. He wasn't sure if he could bring her to within feet of her bed without seriously messing something up otherwise.

And sleeping with Ivy McLain would *seriously* mess something up. She was probably on her way back to California in the morning, or maybe even the day after that, but either way, it didn't matter. He was staying here. Having her and then losing her would probably be worse than never having her at all.

It was fun to go on a date with her. It was a blast, actually. Her enthusiasm when it came to art, her intelligence, her beauty, her laugh…

She was a lethal combination, a drug he couldn't let into his system. He'd tried loving a woman before. He'd loved her for years, and look at how that'd turned out.

No, it was best that he dropped Ivy off and drove away. Away from the temptation, away from her, away from a huge mistake.

Austin was many things, but a player wasn't one of them. A one-night stand wasn't his style.

He put his hand on the gear shift and pushed in the clutch, throwing his truck in reverse.

It was time to go home.

CHAPTER 9

IVY

*I*VY SETTLED DOWN FURTHER into the couch with a groan, wrapping her hands around her mug of coffee. She was *exhausted*. Anyone who'd spent two days talking sense into Iris would be exhausted.

Her sister put the stubborn in McLain.

Huh. Okay, so that didn't make much sense. She sighed and took another sip of her coffee. She obviously needed all the help she could get.

The good news was, after two days of beating on the thick skull that was Iris McLain, Ivy and her mom had finally convinced her that it was best to tell Declan the truth. The *whole* truth. Even the part about how she didn't think she could take care of kids. And the part where medical coding from home was slowly making her blind. Dr. Mor, the local optometrist, had told Iris to either stop coding, or get ready to use a cane *and* a seeing-eye dog for the rest of her life.

Yeah, all of it.

Ivy wasn't always the biggest Declan fan – him leaving her sister for fifteen years without explanation, forcing Ivy to help clean up the mess left behind didn't exactly endear her to him – but…that night of the accident? He'd come to the hospital, petrified. Upset beyond anything she'd ever seen. Declan was normally the most mellow, laid-back human being on the face of the planet, a peacemaker to an extreme. She'd heard through the grapevine that he'd gotten punched more than once when he'd thrown himself between his two warring brothers, stopping a fight with his face, and she had no problems at all believing that story.

On a normal day, he made Gandhi look like a warmonger.

But that night at the hospital? He'd been torn to pieces by what had happened, and by the fact that no one had told him anything. It'd been Iris' call, of course – she'd been the one to insist that no one say a word to him. In fact, Ivy still didn't know how he knew, other than the gossip chain that was Long Valley.

Seeing him in the hospital that night had told Ivy what she needed to know – that he truly did love Iris. Even if they were both too stubborn to admit it, those two were meant to be together.

So, after two days of arguing with Iris, Ivy had finally convinced her of that fact too, which was nothing short of a Christmas miracle, at least in Ivy's eyes.

Speaking of Christmas…

She pulled her phone out and reread the form email from the airline that they'd sent her after she'd called to cancel her flight back to California. The employee had tried to talk to her at the time and warn her about fees and such, but Ivy had been so upset, she hadn't paid much attention.

Any attention, really.

But now…

She scrolled down through the email, dread growing in her stomach. When she'd originally booked her flight up to Idaho, she'd skipped the trip insurance option because it was just one more fee that the airlines liked to tack onto flight prices, and she'd barely been able to afford the base ticket price. In hindsight, not the most brilliant choice she could've made.

The cost of moving her return ticket to another date was almost as much as it would cost to simply buy another ticket. The dread becoming thicker by the moment, she flipped over to the airline app and began scrolling through one-way tickets from Boise to Sacramento going out in the next week.

Thousands. It would cost thousands of dollars.

She began entering in dates further and further away. After Christmas. After New Year's. Finally, she hit dates in the second week of January that were more reasonable, comparatively speaking, of course.

By that point, though, she wouldn't be able to afford even the cheaper ticket price. Her boss, Barry, had let her take the weekend off for her parent's wedding anniversary, after she'd pinky sworn that she'd be back before the rush for the holidays really hit. She'd been booked solid on the calendar in the diner's kitchen until after New Year's.

When Iris had fallen and hurt herself again, she'd texted Barry and pleaded for another week, and he'd begrudgingly given it to her. As the restaurant manager, his focus was on fully staffing the diner for the holiday rush, not on her personal life. Or anyone's personal life. He wasn't exactly well-known for having a heart of gold.

But now…

She wouldn't be able to fly back for a little over a month. Which meant no income that whole time. Which meant no job when she did return, because Barry absolutely wouldn't forgive her being gone that long. Which meant no apartment to return to, because how on earth would she pay January's rent without a paycheck from December?

She stared at her phone, her eyes no longer seeing anything, as the hot tears filled her eyes and then began dripping down her face. Someday, her parents were going to catch onto the fact that their darling younger daughter was not, in fact, going back to California and had, in fact, moved herself right back into their house. They would want to know why. Which means she'd have to fess up to years of white lies and gray lies, and some outright black lies.

Ivy was pretty sure she'd be willing to do almost *anything* to keep from having to do that, but what that "anything" consisted of, she couldn't begin to guess. The easiest thing would be to get a job as a waitress in Sawyer at Betty's Diner, except:

a) Tiffany worked at that diner, which automatically made it a no-go; and

b) Even if Tiffany didn't work there, her parents would surely notice if Ivy suddenly became a waitress at a local restaurant, and they'd want to know why. Surely their uber-successful, hasn't-worked-at-a-restaurant-for-years daughter wouldn't get a job over Christmas simply to pass the time.

Ivy was stuck in the worst pickle of her life, and she didn't have a clue of how to get out of the mess she'd created.

The hot tears trailed ever faster down her face.

CHAPTER 10

AUSTIN

*H*IS HAND HOVERED over his cell phone as he debated with himself. He should call Declan to find out how Iris was doing. It's only neighborly, right? And if the conversation just *happened* to drift toward Ivy, well, that would just be a happy coincidence.

Nothing more than that.

He snatched the phone up and after unlocking it, tapped #1 in his favorites – the *only* phone number listed in his favorites section, and didn't that just say something about him that he didn't exactly want to think about just then – and listened to the phone ring.

Just as he thought it was going to go to voicemail, he heard Declan's deep voice come through.

"Hey Declan! Just calling to find out how Iris is doing." Casual. So very casual. The only way he could be more casual was if he put on swim trunks and perched a pair of sunglasses on top of his head.

"Good, good. She's back at home finally, and is spending a lot of her time resting up. That girl..." Austin could hear the half laugh, half groan come through loud and clear. "I've been thinking about buying her a donkey for Christmas. Just so she knows what it's like to be around someone as stubborn as her."

Austin laughed. That would really only work if Iris bought him a donkey in return. Truly, two people couldn't be more perfectly suited for each other, at least when it came to the Stubborn Scale.

"Oh hey, before I forget: Iris has been bugging me to bug you. She wants you to attend the First Annual Miller/McLain Christmas Party. Since Ivy isn't going back to San Francisco until after the holidays, Iris thought it would be fun to have a big get-together to celebrate. I knew with everything going on with your parents, you probably wouldn't want to go back home for Christmas."

Home. Austin wondered for a moment when North Idaho had stopped feeling like home for him. Was it when he'd first been told his parents were getting a divorce? Or maybe when Monica had mailed his engagement ring back to him so she could start dating Dane, the second richest guy in the county?

Somewhere in there.

He cleared his throat. "Yeah, that'd be good. Christmas Day?"

"Yup. We'll meet over at Stetson's house. He has the biggest house in the family until Wyatt finishes his monstrosity. And anyway, it's the Miller homestead, you know? But, Carmelita will be cooking, so I plan on wearing sweatpants so I can stuff as much down me as possible."

Austin let out a roar of laughter. "Good plan. See you then." After they hung up, Austin stared at his phone.

Ivy was still in town. Why was Ivy still in town? She had a studio and art galleries who would probably love to showcase her paintings over the holidays, not to mention a whole *life* back in California. He'd never expected her to still be here in Long Valley.

But since she was…

His mind ran through the possibilities. What was public, fun to do, and as Christmassy as it comes? After all, they still hadn't seen Tiffany and Ezzy out in public. It was possible that they hadn't gotten the message yet. It was only smart to go on one more date.

Just one more. *Then* he could give Ivy up.

CHAPTER 11

IVY

*I*VY STOOD NEXT TO AUSTIN, his arm wrapped around her as he belted out *God Rest Ye Merry Gentlemen* with the rest of the caroling group. His singing voice was…awful.

Atrocious, really.

He looked down at her and shot her a huge grin and she grinned back, mentally making the note to wear earplugs the next time she went caroling with Austin.

Not that there would be a next time, of course.

She pushed that thought away and glanced

around the Sawyer Retirement Home with a goofy smile plastered to her face. She felt good. Damn good. When they'd arrived at the retirement home for the annual sing-in to the local residents, she'd spotted Tiffany and Ezzy and had stiffened up, her heart racing even as the rest of her body froze in place. Sure, this was the whole point of going on a public date with Austin, but that didn't make it any easier to see her high school tormentors.

But the look on Tiffany's face when she'd glanced over and then had done a double-take when she saw Austin's arm wrapped around Ivy…

Well, that was almost as delicious as when Tiffany and Ezzy marched towards the door, loudly discussing what a lame-ass idea it was to go caroling at a senior citizen's home as a *date*.

Ivy's grin grew even wider as she remembered their snotty comments. That's right – she was on a *date*. With the cutest guy in four counties. Probably four states, actually.

This was a world she was rather happy to inhabit.

The caroling group segued into *It Came Upon a Midnight Clear*, and Ivy sang the lyrics lustily, snuggling into Austin's side. It was coming upon a Christmas Eve soon, and she was thrilled that Austin would be at the First Annual Miller/McLain Christmas Party. Although they wouldn't be there as each other's date, of course – that implied a level of seriousness that just wasn't there after only knowing each other for a couple of weeks – it was still going to be loads of fun.

After New Year's would be when reality intruded, but she was happy to ignore that reality until then, thankyouverymuch. In fact, she was reaching epic levels of avoidance when it came to her financial situation, a talent she hadn't realized she'd possessed until recently.

It Came Upon a Midnight Clear finished up, and Ivy looked towards the caroling director, waiting to hear the name of the next song to sing, when he instead announced that they were done and wished everyone a Merry Christmas. Ivy bit back a twinge of disappointment – she was really starting to enjoy herself. Now she had no excuse to snuggle into Austin's side, which was really too bad.

After some clapping and rounds of hugs, the carolers headed for the door, and out into a great big world of white.

Flakes were falling gently from the sky, blanketing everything as far as the eye could see. To someone else, it might appear magical. To Ivy, it looked evil. Monstrous. This…this *shit* had been what had almost killed her sister. Not to mention that it was just miserable cold.

Why? Why would anyone ever intentionally live in a place where it snowed on a regular basis?!

"Oh wow," Austin breathed, looking out at the white covering the world. "So pretty. You want to walk home? I can come back and get the truck, but I'd love to walk you home in this."

Intentionally…

Her mind ground to a halt. There was no part of this that made any sense whatsoever. He'd have to walk her home, then walk back, then drive home, all so he could spend *more* time outside in the cold and the snow?

Her mouth opened and closed a couple of times, doing a fantastic imitation of a goldfish, but nothing came out. He must've taken her silence as assent because he tucked her arm under his and they took off down the street towards her parents' home.

"That sure was a lot of fun," Austin said cheerfully, every breath creating a cloud around his head that slowly dissipated. The flakes continued to drift down, endlessly down, wrapping them in a world of silence and white. "Thanks for coming with me."

"I really had a blast," Ivy replied. *Except for the part where you're forcing me to walk home in a snowstorm.* But she kept that thought to herself. The flakes swirled around them as they moved slowly down the street, and Ivy had the fleeting thought that it looked like Sawyer had been shoved under the dome of a snow globe, one where God kept shaking it to keep the snow coming.

It was almost a pretty snow, if such a thing could be true, because of how gently it drifted down.

Pretty snow…

Had they slipped alcohol into the hot cocoa they were serving at the retirement home? Ivy couldn't remember *ever* thinking that snow was pretty.

Maybe she was under the influence of a hallucinogenic drug. Maybe she was about to die. Maybe, aliens had taken over her body and she didn't even—

"When are you going back to California?" Austin asked, yanking her out of her thoughts and back into the present. He tucked her arm closer to his side. She shoved her other hand into her coat pocket, wishing again that she had gloves. Or something warmer than what amounted to a fall jacket when it came to Idaho weather. It was her winter jacket in the Bay area, but that didn't mean much up here in the mountains. She tried to hide her teeth-chattering by sheer dint of will.

"Oh, after the new year," she said breezily, as if that thought didn't haunt her every moment of every day. It was more like *Never, because I can't afford to*, but she was still hoping for that Christmas miracle – some way to get out of this predicament she'd found herself in. It hadn't happened yet, but Christmas was still four days away. She was holding out hope. She'd watched *It's a Wonderful Life* every year growing up. She totally believed in Christmas miracles. "I'm staying here until then to spend time with my family. I so rarely get to make it up from California, what with the studio and all; it's fun to spend time with them when I can."

She squinted one eye upward, waiting for the lightning strike to hit. She'd heard of snow lightning. It was a thing. Especially when someone was lying their ever lovin' ass off like she was.

Nothing.

Apparently, God was busy tonight. Not a big surprise, considering the biggest holiday of the year was coming up.

Maybe *that* was as big of a Christmas miracle as she'd be able to expect this year.

"Where are your gloves?" he asked, taking the hand he'd tucked underneath his arm and blowing warm air on it. She quickly pulled her other hand out of her pocket so he could blow on both of them at the same time. She felt prickles of pleasure-pain in her fingers at the warmth.

"I was only supposed to be up here for a few days," she said with a shrug as he tucked both hands underneath his arm. It was a little awkward to walk that way, but heavenly warmth was spreading through her fingers again, so she wasn't about to complain. "I packed light, not thinking I'd be here through multiple snowstorms. Plus, my gloves that I have back at home aren't exactly made for this kind of weather anyway."

Mainly, because California didn't *have* this kind of weather. She thought longingly back towards mid-60s December days, biting back a groan. She missed real human weather so very much. No one should ever intentionally live in this…

This winter wonderland.

Okay, fine, so it was pretty. It didn't mean she had to like it.

"I imagine you don't have any ski resorts in San Francisco?" Austin said with a gentle laugh.

"Not too many," Ivy agreed dryly.

She spotted her parents' house through the white haze. *Almost there.* She was surprised to feel a little sadness at the thought. She'd actually enjoyed walking home in the snow with Austin, something she would've bet body parts on never happening.

Not that she didn't enjoy walking with Austin, of course. It was this dang-blasted beautiful white freezing awful cold shit coming down from the sky that she could do without.

"Thank you for going caroling with me," Austin said after a slight pause. He smiled down at her, joy in his eyes. "I know you're here because of your sister, but...I can't help but be glad for it anyway." They drew to a stop on her parents' front door step, the porch light casting a weak golden glow in the evening darkness. He paused, looking at her and she looked at him and the world swirled around them and she couldn't breathe, oh her heart...

He leaned down and placed his lips on hers, softly, questioningly. Did she want this?

Yes, yes she did.

She slipped her arms around his neck, pulling him closer to her. He groaned, pushing his gloved hands into her damp hair and tilting her head to the side for better access. *Oh, oh…*

His lips were soft and yet demanding as he pulled her to him. His tongue slipped out and ran along the seam of her lips, seeking entrance, and she moaned as she opened her mouth to him. Her heart was beating so hard, she was sure the neighbors would call the police for the noise disturbance, and her mind went blank as she drank in his presence, and then…

And then he pulled away and without a word, headed back out into the snowstorm, down the street, disappearing into the swirling white.

Ivy stared after him, a hand pressed to her lips, surprise thrumming through her. She hadn't expected that kiss, she hadn't expected him to leave abruptly, but most of all, she hadn't expected to want to continue.

A part of her knew that this was a bad idea. They could never work out. Living in different states tended to put a damper on things, but it was more than that. He was a cowboy who worked with local farmers to help them make long-term decisions about what crops to plant and what rotation schedule to follow.

Those weren't talents that were exactly in high demand in the Bay area.

And she couldn't move here. To live back among the people who'd tried so hard to make her life miserable. To live in a world where snow was a regular occurrence six months out of the year. To live where pine trees grew as far as the eye could see, and art for the sake of art wasn't even on anyone's radar.

But despite all of this, she couldn't help the joy running through her as she slipped inside her parents' house and down the hallway to her bedroom. Snuggling up underneath the hot pink comforter that had seemed so awesome when she was a sophomore in high school, she stared up at the ceiling, a loopy grin on her face, playing and replaying the kiss in her mind.

Maybe a Christmas miracle would happen here, too. Maybe she shouldn't give up on it quite yet.

She wrapped the hope for a Christmas miracle around her, snuggled in deep, and drifted off to sleep, a peaceful world of snow continuing to fall gently on Long Valley.

CHAPTER 12

AUSTIN

*H*E PICKED UP THE NEWEST THRILLER by Mark Dawson and stared unseeingly at the pages, then put it down. He automatically went to pick it back up, when his hand froze over the paperback. It was no use. He'd been trying to read that rather short paragraph for the last – he looked at his phone – thirty-two minutes, and still had no idea what it said.

Or what the name of the book was.

He groaned, burying his face in his hands. This was ridiculous. He loved to read. He loved thrillers. He loved Mark Dawson. Austin had long ago taught himself how to entertain himself while alone, because otherwise, he would've gone stark raving mad years ago.

After growing up with Monica practically attached to his hip from their freshman year forward, it'd actually been something he had to consciously teach himself how to do. It was okay to be by himself. It was okay to spend evenings in, with only a book to keep him company.

But today, he couldn't concentrate. Not when he was about to go spend the afternoon at Stetson's house.

Not when he was about to spend the afternoon with *Ivy McLain* at Stetson's house. Because as fun as Stetson was, he was *not* the reason that Austin was having a hard time concentrating.

His eyes flicked towards the ready stack of presents by the front door. He'd bought bottles of wine and boxes of chocolates for everyone, except Ivy. She deserved something more, something special. He'd spent days searching for exactly that, until he'd found the perfect present.

This wasn't a date, of course. You didn't go on a date with a girl, her sister, her parents, and three Miller brothers, wives in tow. Especially not a Christmas Day date. That implied a level of seriousness in their relationship that just wasn't there.

Couldn't be there.

After the holidays, Ivy was going back to California; back to her life in the relative warmth of San Francisco. There, people appreciated her talents, and rewarded her for them. After all, how many people were able to make it financially as a painter? She'd never talked financial specifics with him, of course – it wasn't his place to pry – but to be able to keep a studio and an apartment and live full-time in the Bay area without any outside job meant she was really tearing up the local art scene.

Which she should. She had talent in spades. She'd finally shown him her painting of the Goldfork Mountains that she was working on while up here, and although it had looked amazing to him, she'd been muttering something about how it wasn't quite right. He figured that was just her perfectionism showing itself, because he couldn't see how she could make it any more stunning, but he wasn't about to argue the point with her.

Going back to California...that'd been her appeal from the beginning, of course. She was leaving, and he didn't have to worry about her wanting something more from him. She wouldn't want more, she'd help him get rid of Tiffany in a way that just words couldn't seem to do, and then he could go on with his life. This was why he'd wanted to go on a date with her from day one.

But the last week had been...magical. They went caroling again, sledding out at Stetson's place, and spent a couple of evenings watching old sappy Christmas movies. He started to re-alize that the more time he spent around Ivy, the more he *wanted* to spend around Ivy.

Which was dangerous, but he couldn't seem to help himself.

He pulled himself out of his thoughts and glanced at the deer clock on the wall, the antlers pointing to 12:40. It was time to get going. He hated being late.

Especially being late when it came to seeing Ivy.

He gathered the mountain of gifts into his arms and hooked his foot on the door, pulling it shut behind him. It was time to celebrate Christmas.

CHAPTER 13

IVY

ABBY LEANED OVER TO IVY with a huge grin on her face. "Sooooo…" she said, drawing the word out with relish, "tell us *all.*"

Ivy looked around the group of women, who were all staring right back at her with huge grins on their faces. There was Abby of course, who'd recently married Wyatt (their wedding being where Iris had reunited with Declan), and then there was Jennifer, Stetson's new wife, their even newer baby bouncing on her shoulder, and last but certainly not least, Iris herself. They'd all managed to find *the* guy they were supposed to be with, while Ivy…

Well, she was just play-acting with Austin. It was embarrassing to admit, even if just to herself, that it was all for show. Who pretended to date a guy to get revenge on their high school nemesis? What did that say about her?

Of course, there was the fact that neither Tiffany nor Ezzy would've ever spotted them during their Christmas movie marathon three days ago, so that made the efficacy of their "show" somewhat questionable, but Ivy studiously ignored that fact.

The girls were all *still* staring at her. Ivy gulped.

"He seems like a real sweetie," Abby said, sensing her discomfort at being on the receiving end of so much interest, and trying to gently guide her towards safer ground. "He's not from around here, right?"

Ivy smiled, feeling relief course through her at having something simple and straightforward to discuss with them. Something that didn't include *love* or *relationship*. "No, he came from up north – up in the panhandle. He took over the extension office when Mr. Snow retired."

Austin had been at that job for two years now, but that didn't keep everyone in Long Valley from considering him the new guy. He'd probably be the new guy right up until the day he retired.

Jennifer nodded sagely. "Stets has been saying that Austin's been a real big help in getting a new crop rotation figured out. Do you think you two will continue to date even after you go back to—oh hello!"

Everyone turned to look, even Ivy, even as she was inwardly begging God that it was not, in fact, Austin behind her.

It was.

She met his gaze.

He sent her a huge grin. He knew they'd been talking about him.

She sent him a weak smile in return. She'd been caught.

She was pretty sure her hair and face were *exactly* the same color. Damn fair skin, anyway.

His grin got wider.

She glared at him.

He bust out laughing.

She glared harder.

"Oh, the magic of the Miller homestead," Carmelita said in her thick Hispanic accent as she came bustling into the living room with another plate of Christmas cookies. These appeared to be sugar cookies with frosting, at least according to Ivy's super-sensitive-cookie-finding nose. "Every Christmas, someone falls in love here in this house. It is Mr. and Mrs. Miller, watching over us, God bless their souls." She made the sign of the cross over her ample chest as she placed the cookies on the coffee table – sugar cookies indeed – scooting it a half inch to the right, and then straightening up. Sending Ivy a guileless grin, she sashayed back into the kitchen, leaving behind a roomful of laughing females.

It was Austin's turn to look like he'd swallowed a frog.

It rather served him right, in Ivy's not-so-humble opinion.

"Let me drool over your adorable baby," Ivy said in an obvious bid to change the subject, holding her arms out for Flint. She was quite sure she'd never seen such a picture-perfect baby in all her life, and anyway, Jennifer owed her for embarrassing her in front of Austin.

She felt, rather than saw, Austin move away. He was probably going to head out into the barn to hang out with the guys until mealtime. Jennifer handed Flint over along with a burp cloth, and Ivy began patting and rocking him as she looked around, realizing Juan was absent, too. He was the ten-year-old soon-to-be-adopted son of Wyatt and Abby, and as the only kid in the family other than Flint, it was probably hard for him to figure out where he should hang out.

Well, the barn was a good choice. The guys would pretend to work on a tractor or combine or something, but everyone knew they were just out there to hide from Carmelita bossing them around to set up more tables or chairs.

She snuggled Flint closer to her. He felt wonderful in her arms; a bundle of squishy love. She looked over at Jennifer with a huge grin on her face. "He's so beautiful," she cooed.

Flint gurgled. Jennifer beamed. Iris grinned.

Ivy narrowed her eyes at that one. No, no, no. She was *not* baby hungry. She could read Iris' expression from a mile away, and she did *not* appreciate the direction her sister's thoughts had taken.

Ivy simply thought that Flint was cute. That just meant she had eyeballs in her head, nothing more.

At Ivy's glare, Iris smothered her grin and, with a teasing glint in her eye that didn't bode well for Ivy, turned to their mom. She was carrying in a bowl of punch from the kitchen to deliver to the buffet table. Carmelita had declared that their mom could help her in the kitchen, but hadn't let anyone else in thus far.

Ivy's nose twitched again. Stuffing. There was definitely stuffing in the turkey.

"Mom, don't you think that Ivy is just about the cutest mother you ever did see?" Iris asked in an overly sweet, syrupy voice.

She was *such* a sister sometimes.

Their mom looked up from the punch-bowl arranging and sent Iris a warning glance. "Now dear, I think that Ivy will make a splendid mother, if and when she ever chooses to have children."

In other words, she knew Iris was trying to make Ivy blush, and even though she'd succeeded – damn her Irish roots – Ivy had won the war. Mom had sided with her. She stuck her tongue out at Iris. Iris laughed.

Ivy rolled her eyes…and then laughed too.

It was good to be home. Even if it meant that she was stuck there indefinitely, in that moment, Ivy wasn't sure that she would trade it for the world. She'd missed her family and being teased and beautiful baby boys while she'd been hiding out in California, trying to pretend that she loved abstract expressionism.

She stopped short, her head snapping up. Abby noticed the movement out of the corner of her eye and looked over. "You okay?" she asked.

Ivy nodded and sent her an overly bright smile. "Yes, yes, of course," she said, a bit too loudly. Abby cocked her head to the side, obviously not buying it. Ivy ignored that and continued to bounce Flint as she thought through that again.

Trying to *pretend* that she loved abstract art? She didn't *pretend* to love it. It was her life. She'd focused on it ever since she'd moved to San Francisco and had first started taking courses at the California College of the Arts. Her art teachers had rhapsodized about the flow and curves and beauty, and as Ivy had sat in class, staring at the paintings being projected up on the wall, she'd fallen in love with the style right along with them.

Much better than being a landscape artist, anyway. Painting a couple of mountains was *easy*. Abstract art was *hard*. You had to put your heart and soul into it, not just replicate what was in front of you.

Which was strange, now that she thought about it, because she sure was struggling with her painting of the Goldfork Mountains, which wasn't supposed to be anything more than a keep-busy project. She'd been sketching the view that day that Austin had run into her out in the woods, and had started painting it after her dad had found her oils up in the attic.

But no matter how much she worked on the painting, it was never *quite* right. Maybe it was the sky. She'd painted it as a sunset, so maybe she needed to add some more ora—

"Ivy!" her mother practically shouted.

Okay, did shout.

Ivy jerked her head up. "What?" she asked, dazed.

"It's time for dinner, and Jennifer would probably like her baby back now."

Ivy looked down at Flint, nestled against her shoulder, fast asleep, and up to Jennifer, who was holding her arms out for him, a smile dancing on her lips. Ivy flushed red again – being a redhead just wasn't all it was cracked up to be some days – and quickly held Flint up to her.

"I'd marry him if I were you," Jennifer whispered in her ear as she scooped Flint up, then pulled back and winked at her. "If he makes you that oblivious to the world…" She let the sentence trail off and headed to the table.

Ivy looked over at the table. *Whoops.*

Everyone was there, and they were all waiting for her to move her ass over to it.

The thing was, she hadn't been lost in her thoughts, thinking about Austin. She'd been thinking about paintings, which was only right. The art world was where she belonged.

Not Long Valley.

After a scrumptious dinner that left Ivy feeling overstuffed and very, very happy, the whole family moved into the living room, with couples sitting everywhere they could shoehorn themselves into, and Juan sitting on the floor, gingerly holding a sleeping Flint. Ivy grinned at the scene, loving it. He already seemed to be fitting into the family, even if he didn't seem to be quite sure of what to do with a sleeping eight month old.

He hadn't said much that day, at least that Ivy had heard, but when he looked at Abby and Wyatt, he had stars in his eyes.

Ivy looked to her left; her whole body was squished up against the side of Austin, who was smiling down at her. He was obviously very happy with the seating arrangement. She couldn't pretend she minded it, no matter what her brain kept warning her to think. She'd worry about their relationship and painting styles and nagging feelings about unfinished landscape paintings later.

Right now was *Christmas*.

Declan busied himself, distributing the presents spilling out from under the tree, and the sound of tearing paper filled the air, along with shouts of glee and thank-yous. Ivy looked around, her smile slowly fading as the truth she'd been avoiding bonked her over the head again. No matter what she'd been telling herself to focus on, the painful truth was in front of her: She hadn't provided a single present under that tree.

She'd wanted to. *Oh*, how she'd wanted to. But she couldn't get back home; she couldn't pay her rent; she couldn't even buy herself a pair of gloves to make it through this dang-blasted winter.

She could only hope no one noticed the lack of presents from her. She would simply die if someone brought it up, she was sure of it.

"Here you go," Austin said softly in her ear, placing a long, thin box in her hands. A simple gold ribbon was wrapped around the middle, providing the only wrapping for the present.

Ivy stared down at it in shock. What on earth was it? She looked up at Austin and he smiled back, close enough that she could clearly see the brown flecks in his otherwise-brilliant green eyes.

Did he have…love in his eyes? It couldn't be love. He couldn't love her. She was imagining things.

She looked back down at the box, the rest of the world falling away. Tugging at the gold ribbon, she lifted the lid and—

"Oh!" she gasped, her hand flying to cover her mouth. Inside of the box lay a pair of leather gloves, nestled in tightly. She gently pulled them out, running her hands over the buttery soft leather. "Oh Austin," she said, her throat tight with emotion. They were beautiful, so damn beautiful.

"They reminded me of you," he said softly. "Classic, simple, soft, and beautiful." He shrugged, looking embarrassed that he'd waxed so poetic. "Well anyway, since you've been stuck up here without your gloves for so long, I thought you'd like 'em."

She threw her arms around him, hugging him tight. "Like them?" she pushed out. She felt her eyes tearing up a little and she blinked rapidly, trying to will the tears away. "I *love* them."

She pulled them on, the cashmere lining soft and smooth against her skin. She closed her eyes in ecstasy. She was pretty sure she'd never felt something so sinfully soft as these gloves. She opened her eyes and looked up at him. "Thank you," she whispered. She leaned up and planted a quick kiss on his lips, which rapidly turned into…something more. The whooping and hollering finally broke through the haze surrounding her and she pulled back, her face afire once more.

This time, though, Austin's face matched hers. Which was only fair.

As she showed off the gloves to Iris, who ooh'd and ahh'd over them, she heard Carmelita sniffle, "It is so good to have my boys under the same roof this year. Mr. and Mrs. Miller would be so happy, bless their souls." Ivy shot Iris a questioning look, and Iris sent back an answering one – *I'll tell you later.*

Sometimes, it was nice to have a sister.

Sometimes.

Declan passed Iris her present, pulling Iris' attention away, and Ivy watched with morbid curiosity. Was he going to propose to her right here in front of everyone? The box looked a little large, but Ivy wouldn't put it past Declan to give Iris a rock the size of a baseball, just so everyone knew she was his. After his stunt fifteen years ago, Ivy hadn't thought she'd ever forgive him, but now? She couldn't ignore the love on his face. Yeah, maybe he'd made mistakes in the past, but it was time to move on. Iris had, and Ivy needed to trust her sister's judgment.

Not to mention that Declan only had eyes for her. They followed Iris' every movement as she opened the box and then gasped with pleasure. "Thank you!" she exclaimed, pulling some colored, cut stones out of the box.

"I bought these stones from the same company that Great-Grandpa Miller worked for when he first moved to Long Valley in the 1800s," Declan said proudly as Iris ooh'd and ahh'd over each one. "We're not called the Gem State for nothin', you know. I thought you could use them in the canes when you carve them."

"Thank you, thank you, thank you," Iris said, throwing her arms around him and kissing him with joy.

And kissing, and kissing, and kissing.

Ivy couldn't stop laughing. After having been on the other end of this scene just minutes before, it was rather delightful to see her sister fall into the same trap.

Finally, they pulled apart and Iris collapsed against Declan's chest, her face a nice brilliant red. Ivy grinned in delight.

Yes, revenge was sweet.

Next to her, Austin was laughing. "So you've finally figured out how to kiss a girl, eh?" he said to Declan.

"Ohhhh…this sounds like a story I want to hear," Ivy piped up.

Her mom said, "Yes please!" while her dad tried to shush her.

But Austin wouldn't be stopped anyway. He was on a roll and was going to have some fun at his best friend's expense.

"So there we were, on a double date up at the University of Idaho. Declan here is paired up with some really cute girl, but he doesn't seem to be into her much. Probably because she doesn't have red hair and blue eyes." He winked at Iris, who flushed red again. "At the end of the night, we're dropping off our dates, and this girl goes up on her tippy toes for a kiss. Declan here dodges her and pecks her on the cheek instead. Mumbles something about how he won't kiss a girl in public, even though it was pitch-dark outside and no one could've seen 'em!"

As the laughter roared, Ivy looked over at Juan, who looked half-thrilled to be included in such adult talk, and simultaneously embarrassed to death. According to Abby, he would be eleven soon, which meant he was about to discover that girls were really, really cool.

As handsome as he was, Ivy was pretty sure

Abby and Wyatt would have to fend off said girls with a baseball bat.

"Well," Declan drawled as soon as the laughter finally let up, "you aren't the public – you're family!"

Everyone bust out laughing again, but this time, Ivy was the one mortified. Did this mean that Declan was planning on proposing to Iris? And did he think Austin would propose to her?

It was *way* too soon in their relationship to be talking about marriage. Ivy gulped hard. Maybe Declan knew something she didn't. Maybe Austin was getting a lot more serious about her than she'd realized.

She chanced a glance up at him and saw him grinning and laughing as he and Declan exchanged friendly insults. No, it'd been a joke. Nothing more.

Which she was happy about.

Very happy.

CHAPTER 14

AUSTIN

*H*E LOOKED DOWN at his wobbling knees and back up at Ivy. "You think this is a good idea, huh?" he said doubtfully.

It really didn't seem like it to him.

She skated in circles around him, her laughter spilling out. "C'mon, just push forward a little. It's actually easier to stay upright if you're moving. Like a bike, except—"

"Except here, I have thin metal blades between me and death?" he interrupted.

Ivy let out a huge laugh at that one, her cheeks a rosy red color, her eyes sparkling in the dim winter lighting. She was brightening up this dark and dreary winter day just by being her. He wondered if she realized what a gift that was.

"Yeah, death," she said dryly when she finally calmed down enough to speak. "Do you want me to ask the front staff how many have died while ice skating this past year?"

"No, no, I'm willing to participate in this death-defying stunt," he said airily, as if bestowing a great gift upon her. "But only if you'll take my hand and help me."

She skated a little closer, and then flipped around and started skating backwards. "You want me to hold your hand?" she said teasingly. "Don't boys have cooties? I'm pretty sure I learned that somewhere."

He pushed forward a little, his ankles shaking almost as much as his knees. He was missing Bob just then. Horses were easy. Ice skating was scary. He didn't care how Ivy made it look; he knew the truth.

"Hold on," he said, puffing as he tried to keep up with her, "I thought you said you didn't have an athletic bone in your body! Were you sandbagging me, so I'd agree to go ice skating with you?"

Her laughter tinkled out again. "I guess I didn't consider ice skating to be athletic," she admitted with a shrug as she did a quick twirl in front of him. "It's *balls* that get me. They fly at me and smack me in the face and break my glasses and they're just horrible little objects."

"Glasses?" he asked between pants. They were almost to the other side of the rink, where he could grab onto the railing and rest for a minute. Whoever said that ice skating wasn't a sport – *ahem, Ivy* – was obviously in better shape than he was. His thighs were burning from the strain of trying to keep upright. "I didn't know you wore glasses."

"Contacts now. But yup, glasses *and* braces all through junior high and part of high school. Would you believe they had me in braces for four years? My tormentors weren't especially bright, and so they stuck with nicknames like 'Metal Mouth' and 'Four Eyes.' Heaven forbid they strain themselves in the creativity department..."

She shot him a brilliant smile, showing off her gorgeous and very straight white teeth. He had a hard time imagining anyone teasing her based on her appearance. She was so damn beautiful. His eyes drifted down her body, which she was showcasing to perfection with a drapy sweater thingy that clung to her generous curves.

Damn beautiful.

They'd made it! He grabbed onto the railing that encircled the ice skating rink and stood still for a moment, happy to be upright and stable.

She skated up to him and then stopped abruptly, spraying him with ice shavings. "You know what movie we should watch tonight?" she asked rhetorically as she skated back and forth next to him, waiting not-so-patiently for him to recuperate. "*The Cutting Edge.*"

He furrowed his brow. "I'm not sure I've—"

She held out her hands for him, and he took them, placing his trust in her to keep him upright.

"I'm not sure I've heard of it," he finished as she began skating backwards, pulling him for-ward like a small child on training wheels. She was wearing his Christmas present today, and he had to admit, she did it with style. She made those gloves look good.

She made everything look good.

Skating with a soft-on was probably not helping matters.

"Never…" she stuttered, staring at him with horror as she easily navigated them around the curve of the rink and into the straightaway. "Well! I know what we're doing tonight. Never watched *The Cutting Edge*," she muttered under her breath with disgust. "What did you do during the 90s? Live under a rock?"

Pretty much.

But he wasn't about to say that out loud.

They did a few more laps around the skating rink, enjoying it all to themselves except a father-son pair off to the side who were busy trying to keep each other upright. Both of them seemed to be able to ice skate as well as Austin…which was to say, not at all.

They needed an Ivy.

The world was better with Ivys around.

His heart twisted at that thought, because he

knew he'd be losing her soon. She'd be returning to California after New Year's, which was just five more days.

Thankfully, one of the benefits of being an extension agent was that not too many farmers and ranchers were planning next year's crop and animal rotation between Christmas and New Year's. This meant that Austin could take the week off without anyone caring a bit. He'd normally take the week to catch up on paperwork — that's what he did last year, anyway — but he was losing Ivy soon. He'd much rather spend the week with her. Paperwork would always be there.

Ivy would not.

His heart twisted again.

"You okay?" Ivy asked, breaking into his thoughts.

"Oh yeah, of course!" he said brightly, and then realized that he sounded overly dramatic. Like he was trying too hard.

Which he was, but he wasn't supposed to sound like it.

"You just looked like you swallowed a live

frog," Ivy said, smiling as always, but her eyes revealed her worry. They were scanning his face, just like his were scanning hers.

"A live frog, eh?" he asked jovially. Dammit, he was not doing a good job of playing it cool here.

"You know, like...*ribbit?*" She made the sound of a croaking frog.

A sick, malnourished frog.

He mock-glared at her. "That is *not* what a frog sounds like," he informed her. "It needs more gusto, more from the gut." He pulled his hands away unthinkingly to gesture at his stomach, which meant no more Ivy holding him up.

His arms started pinwheeling and his forward momentum carried him right into Ivy and they were crashing into each other and down to the ground and he threw himself underneath her, trying to save her from hitting the ice, which meant she hit his lungs instead. The air whooshed out of him as the world went a little black around the edges, and he kept blinking, trying to bring the world back into focus and she was staring down at him, her mouth moving but nothing coming out.

Finally, her voice started to filter in. "If you don't talk to me in the next six seconds, I'm going to drag you to the ER," Ivy yelled at the top of her lungs.

Right next to his head.

He looked up at her and tried to focus on her face, swimming around in front of him. "I can hear you," he said, a lopsided grin on his face.

"You can…" she sputtered. "First Iris and now you – I don't think I could handle someone else with a brain injury!"

He pulled her down on top of him, snuggling her against him. "I think you should kiss me all better," he said as he felt himself harden against the curves of her body. She glared down at him, indecisive about her response. She wanted to yell at him more – it was written all over her face – but she was also beginning to see the humor in the situation.

"You sure are needy," she breathed as she

inched closer, the *wanting to kiss him* part apparently winning out.

Thank God.

"You're the one who promised me that this wasn't a death-defying feat," he reminded her, their lips just a hair-breadths apart. "I think a kiss to make me all better isn't so much to ask."

"Mmmm..." she murmured, her eyes drifting shut. "I like how you think."

He pulled her a little closer, her lips opening up as she began to melt into him. She flicked her tongue out, inviting him to come in to play, and he chased her tongue back into her mouth, tasting hot chocolate and joy. He started to harden even more while his mind began to wander into naughty territory. What did her gorgeous curves look like in a pair of bra and panties? If they were a light beige color, edged with lace, she would look like she was wearing nothing at all.

He wanted to explore every curve and swell, memorizing her body before—

"You two need help?" a voice asked,

breaking in. Ivy jerked away, shoving an elbow into his side as she tried to scramble off him.

"*Oof,*" he grunted at the same time that Ivy said gaily, "Oh no, we're fine!" She was straightening her sweater and adjusting her scarf. "Just fine!"

Austin sat up gingerly, rubbing his side *and* head, and looked up at the pimply-and-oh-so-bored teenager standing over them. "We're good," he told him. "Just getting up now."

The employee sent them a look that clearly said *And no kissing while you're doing it!* before turning to head towards the pay booth to hunker back down with his iPhone, if their entrance into the ice skating rink was anything to judge by. Austin was surprised the teen had looked up from his phone long enough to notice them kissing, although, thinking about it, they had been kissing for quite a while.

After the teen left, Ivy looked at him, and instead of being mortified, she was grinning hugely.

"Why are you so happy?" he asked absent-mindedly while considering the best way to get to his feet. He finally decided that flipping over onto his hands and knees and trying to stand up from that position seemed the least likely way to get himself killed in the process. After some scrabbling at the ice and then a hand up from Ivy, which he wasn't too prideful to take, he was on his feet.

"Do you know what Teenage Ivy would've done to get caught making out by the ice skating rink employee? Probably a good thing no one offered it to me as a possibility. I hate to think about what I would've been willing to do."

"Didn't get kissed a lot when you were a teen, huh?" Austin asked as they slowly made their way towards the exit.

"If by 'not a lot,' you mean 'pretty much never,' then yeah. That often." She sent him a laughing grin.

He shook his head in disbelief as they sat down on the bench to change into street shoes and return their rented ice skates. "So are all the guys in Long Valley blind as a bat?" he asked as he pulled the laces loose and wiggled his feet out.

"Four Eyes and Metal Mouth, remember?

And even after I got contacts and my braces were removed, all of the guys already 'saw' me. You know? They'd known me since I was in kindergarten. They didn't bother looking at the new me." She shrugged. "And anyway, if you'd met Teenage Ivy, you probably wouldn't have liked her either. I was a snob sometimes."

Street shoes on, they wandered back out, returning their rentals to the booth as they passed, the teenage boy not even bothering to look up from his phone.

Ivy rolled her eyes, and Austin wasn't sure if that was at her teenage self or the teenage boy.

"I was going to be an *artist*." She said the word with a French accent and then wrinkled her nose at him. "Truthfully, it was easier to reject the kids before they could reject me. It hurt less that way." They climbed into his truck, which he turned on to warm up while he continued to listen to her. Although he knew she was telling him the truth, it was still hard to wrap his mind around the description she was giving, versus the woman in front of him. "Kids can be cruel, and I never really fit in here," she said softly. "Considering I was born and raised here, that was really hard. It took me a good long while to figure out where I belonged. Who I was. What I cared about."

She shrugged, looking out the fogged-up window, refusing to meet his eye as she talked. "I think the hardest part of all was living in Iris' shadow. She was everything I wasn't. Popular. Loved. Smart. Tall. Athletic. People didn't shove her into lockers or into toilets."

He let the silence stretch out between them as she stared and stared out the passenger side window. Finally, she turned towards him, her eyes suspiciously bright. "Well anyway," she said, her voice scratchy. She cleared it and tried it again. "Life in Sawyer wasn't always easy, but that's why I left. Being an adult, I could." She shrugged. "I just had to wait my time."

He nodded slowly, putting the truck in reverse and pulling out of the parking spot. They headed out of the parking lot and back onto the main highway that stretched between Franklin and Sawyer.

He didn't say anything. He didn't really

know what to say. In a lot of ways, their lives were exact opposites from each other. Growing up was wonderful for him. Perfect in practically every way. It wasn't until he left for college that his life fell apart.

Ivy's life, on the other hand, didn't really start until college.

It was funny to look at the world that way.

He stayed silent. If she wanted to talk, he'd let her. He would listen to whatever she needed to tell him.

"I wanted to kill myself," she said softly. So softly he wasn't quite sure he'd heard her right. *Surely* that wasn't what she'd said. He took a quick peek at her and the look on her face…

He had heard her right.

Before he could say anything – *was* there anything to be said to statements like that? – she continued on. "I was too much of a wimp. I sat in the art closet after school – I don't know where Mrs. Henderson was at that day – and thought about ending it all. I debated my choices. Hanging. Pills. My dad's handgun. Where I'd do it. When I'd do it.

"And then, I stood up and went home and pretended nothing was wrong. Because I couldn't actually kill myself. If I were more brave, I probably would have. If there'd been a way to do it where I wouldn't feel any pain – I'd just go to sleep and never wake up – I'm sure I would've done it. I just wanted to disappear, but I didn't want to cause Iris and my parents any pain, so I wanted to disappear *completely*.

"I watched *It's a Wonderful Life* every year at Christmas, so I knew that the world would be worse off without me. Blah blah blah. But I didn't believe it. I just didn't want my parents to have to wonder where they went wrong.

"So in the end, I did nothing at all. Well, except move to San Francisco. I did that graduation night."

Austin gathered his thoughts, trying to marshal them into some semblance of order. He had to let her know that it wasn't okay, what she went through. That she wasn't a wimp. That to choose life was hard, damn hard, and she should be proud of herself for doing it.

But before he could get his words lined out,

she said softly, "I had only come home once since graduation, before this trip up here. I was doing my very best to pretend that Sawyer didn't exist, Long Valley didn't exist, Idaho didn't exist. When people asked me where I was from, I'd usually give them some flip answer about having lived a lot of places, which wasn't true. I'd lived in Sawyer, Idaho and in San Francisco, California. That's it. But I didn't want to claim Idaho, not even in passing. But…"

She took in a deep breath, and she turned to him in her seat, sending him a genuine smile this time.

"But I'm glad I came. I'm glad I met you."

He reached out across the console, and took her hand in his. "Me too," he said softly.

He would tell her everything later – how proud he was of her, making it through this life that hadn't been kind to her. How beautiful he thought she was, inside and out. How happy he was to have met her.

But for now, he'd simply hold her hand, and be there for her.

CHAPTER 15

IVY

*I*VY GUIDED HER HORSE, a beautiful palomino, down the rocky path carefully. Large stones plus deep snow weren't a good combination for the health of a horse, especially considering the fact that she was pretty sure that Adam Whitaker, the vet in town and owner of said palomino, would actually want her back in one piece.

Strange how that worked.

"It's beautiful out here today," Austin said over his shoulder to her.

"It really is," Ivy said wonderingly. She had

borrowed Iris' warm winter jacket for this outing, along with some long johns and wool socks, and it was amazing what a difference that made to her mental state of being. It was bizarre to think that she was enjoying a horse ride in the dead of winter in Sawyer, Idaho, but...

She was.

She tightened her hands around the reins, looking down at the beautiful gloves Austin had given her. She found herself staring at them often – they were quite possibly the most gorgeous gloves she'd ever laid eyes on. Iris whispered to her that she'd heard through the grapevine (meaning Declan, of course) that Austin had spent a couple hundred dollars on them.

That seemed crazy to Ivy – who had that kind of money to put down on Christmas presents?! – but the quality of the gloves made Ivy believe the price tag was real. They felt like heaven, wrapped around her hands.

"Are you getting cold?" Austin asked, pulling her out of her thoughts.

She looked at him, squinting against the glare of the sun off the snowdrifts. Next time, she needed to wear her sunglasses.

There will be no next time.

She pushed that depressing thought away and sent Austin a cheerful grin instead. "Nope, I'm good. Why do you ask?"

"You were staring down at your hands," he said with a low chuckle. "I thought you were trying to send beams of heat at them with your eyeballs."

She threw back her head and laughed. "Don't I wish that was how it worked," she said, still laughing. "Us wimpy California girls would appreciate that superpower, that's for sure."

He tossed her a sexy grin over his shoulder. Not intentionally sexy; just sexy because it was Austin. He probably looked good enough to eat with a spoon after working a cattle drive for a week straight. He had those kinds of genetics. It just wasn't fair.

"Hmmm…superpower. You'd waste a superpower on keeping your hands warm?" he asked teasingly. The trail widened out a little, and she nudged her horse forward to pull it up even with Bob. Austin stabled his horse out at Adam's place, so it'd been a quick trip to trailer them both up and bring them out here into the national forest.

"Waste?" she repeated saucily. "You are obviously an Idaho boy if you think it's a 'waste' to keep your hands warm. And anyway, I'd use my heat beams on other things too. No more cold feet! And if I could really turn up the power, I could cook dinner with just my eyes." She looked at him and batted her eyelashes. "Seems like a damn good idea to me!"

He laughed, and she unthinkingly reached over and put her hand on his arm as she chuckled with him. He looked down at her hand and then up at her. Their gazes caught and the air crackled around them. Tomorrow was New Year's Eve, and Ivy knew how she wanted to ring in the new year.

She cleared her throat. "So, you didn't say what you wanted as your superpower," she said huskily.

"Hmmm…" He pretended to think deeply about the question, as if his life depended on the answer.

"I mean, other than light beams coming out of your eyes. *Obviously*, that would be the best superpower, but since I already have that one, you have to pick another one."

"Is that how it works?" he said quietly, laughing.

"Of course! Haven't you paid any attention to the Marvel universe? Not a single character has the same superpower. That would just be boring. *Duh.*" She gave that last word her best Valley Girl flair, which earned her another laugh from Austin.

"Well…" he said contemplatively, "I guess I'd pick the superpower of being able to go back in time. Time traveler."

Her first instinct was to tease him – that sounded like a lamer superpower than heat beams from her eyeballs so she could cook dinner easily – but as she looked over at him, her breath caught. She didn't know what was causing that look on his face, but somewhere along the way, Austin had become serious on her.

"So why do you want to become a time traveler?" she asked softly. He'd listened to her yesterday; it was only fair she listened to him today.

It surely couldn't be any worse of a story than hiding in the art closet at the high school and bawling your eyes out while contemplating suicide. She was pretty sure that particular story won the Shitty Story Contest.

She'd never told anyone that story, not even Iris, and having him listen yesterday…it meant a lot to her. She felt better. Freer. Lighter.

She wanted to offer the same support to Austin.

She waited patiently – not usually one of her strong suits – while he mulled through what he was going to say. He wasn't someone to blurt things out – unlike her – and so she'd learned over the past month to wait longer and be more patient with him. Rather than taking silence to mean he had nothing to say, she'd learned to take silence to mean that he was still thinking about what to say.

Which was a totally different thing.

His brow furrowing, he looked off through the trees and rocky hillsides. "Monica Klaunche and I dated for five years. For the record, that's one more year than Declan and Iris dated before Declan contracted temporary insanity and broke up with Iris for fifteen years. Well, so maybe not temporary, but definitely insane."

Ivy laughed softly, but just kept watching his face closely. The idea of him dating someone else for five years was oddly painful, but wherever this chick was now, she was obviously not still Austin's girlfriend.

Not that Ivy had any say over who Austin did or didn't date. She would be heading back to California soon.

Or would be as soon as she could figure out how to pay for a plane ticket.

He let out a sigh, drawing Ivy back into the present. "Monica had always been this sweet girl – big smile, friendly to everyone, and I thought I was in love. You can't be with someone for five years without thinking it's true love. We were going to wait until I graduated from college and took over my dad's farm before getting married. I wanted to be able to provide for her, you know?"

He snuck a quick glance at Ivy, maybe to check if she was listening? Ivy leaned over and squeezed his arm, her silent affirmation that she was indeed listening to him. She didn't want to derail him from his thoughts with words, though, instead choosing to simply be there.

Sometimes, you just needed someone to hear you.

"We graduated from high school and then… she didn't want to go to the University of Idaho with me. Told me she wanted to stay back at home and just take a year off from school. She was burnt out on it.

"I understood, but it was hard because home was an hour away from the U of I, which meant an hour trip each way through deep snow in the dead of winter if I wanted to come home and visit her. I won't lie and claim that I was thrilled with her decision, but I understood it."

The trail narrowed for a moment, so Austin

slowed down, letting Ivy go in front and duck under a few low-lying pine tree branches before they met up again on the other side. He continued, "One visit back home, my mom was acting weird. Her face was all red and her eyes were swollen and she just looked like shit, you know? I mean, I won't pretend that I'm the most observant person on the face of the planet, but she just looked awful. When I asked where Dad was, she said he was back East, visiting relatives. Which was weird, because we don't have any relatives back East, but she just clammed up after that. Wouldn't answer a thing. It was like trying to nail jello to the wall."

He let out a little laugh that turned into a sigh. "The next weekend, I came home again because even though it'd been a week, I hadn't gotten any closer to getting an answer. I thought if I came home, I could demand an answer in person. Force the issue. I hadn't had any luck the week before; I don't know why I thought I'd have more luck the next week. Naïveté, I guess."

He shrugged.

Her heart broke. She too had believed that life would always get better; that the bullies would finally leave her alone; that she'd finally be able to quit working as a waitress; that she'd…

Well, that she would be able to magically pay for a plane ticket back home.

Yeah, Ivy was the Queen of Naïveté.

"I heard them yelling before I even got out of the car. I was so confused. There's my dad's treasured guitar, lying out in the snow in the front yard. Out sails a painting of my dad when he was a toddler. The frame broke and scattered.

"I slammed the door of the car and took off running for the front door. I don't know what I thought I could do – save my parent's house from the thief who was apparently destroying things instead of just stealing them? I was in shock, and acting purely on instinct. If I could just get in the front door, I could make things better. Make things right.

"My parents turned and looked at me when I came running in, and we just stared at each other for a minute. I hadn't told them I was coming home, and the shock of me showing up in the middle of their fight scared them into silence."

He took a deep, haggard breath, rubbing the back of his neck as he stared off through the wintry woods. "They were getting a divorce. My dad had been cheating on my mom for years, and she'd finally caught him. All of the stupid, cliché stuff that you hear about but you don't think would actually happen to *your* family? My dad admitted to it all. He'd been sleeping with the bookkeeper for our family farm. I'd always thought that she seemed a little too…friendly. Attached. Familiar with my father. But I didn't know. I didn't think…"

He took another deep breath and looked at Ivy. "You're a really good listener," he said quietly with a small chuckle that quickly died on his lips. "I didn't mean to tell you all of this. I don't tell people this very often."

Ivy was pretty sure he meant, "Absolutely never," but she didn't say that. Instead, she squeezed his hand and said softly, "I'm hear to listen to whatever you want to say."

He nodded slowly. "It wasn't enough that this destroyed my family. One fell swoop, and my home and my parents...all of it was wrecked. No, it got much worse than that." He sent her a tight smile. "I was once the heir to the largest spread in Kootenai County. I bet you didn't know you were on a date with such a rich guy."

"I honestly had no idea," she said with a laugh, "but now that I know..." She winked at him.

His smile quickly disappeared. "I was the only kid. My parents struggled to conceive, and were lucky to even have me. My parents raised me, secure in the knowledge that I had a future. They insisted I go to college and get a bachelor's degree, but once I did, the farm was mine. Lock, stock, and barrel. My parents had a small cabin that they were going to retire to. I'd give them a stipend every year until they died, as my payment for the farm, but the farm itself would be mine. That's why I wasn't willing to take that year off from college with Monica. She'd wanted me to, but I wanted to finish college and get on with the rest of my life, you know?

"Except, once my father's infidelity was discovered and my parents started the process of getting a divorce, things got really ugly really fast. The belongings on the front lawn were only the beginning. Quickly, they devolved into physical fights and the judge ordered them to have no contact with each other outside of the courtroom, except through their attorneys. Neither parent acted better than the other one; they were both awful."

His mouth pinched, and Ivy knew that wherever this was going, it was about to get there, and it wasn't going to be pretty when it happened.

"The judge ordered the farm sold and the proceeds divided between my parents. They couldn't agree how to settle it otherwise, so it was just sold instead. And with it, my inheritance disappeared. They didn't offer to give me part of the sale of the farm so I could buy another one; they couldn't even agree to let me buy it from them. It went to some ten-gallon hat wannabe who drove the farm into the ground within three years. It went up on the auction block last spring. That was a rough day."

He let out a bitter laugh. "And yet, that isn't even all."

Ivy drew in a sharp breath at that. How was that not all? What else could there poss—

Oh. Monica Something Or Another. He still hadn't explained why he wasn't married to his childhood sweetheart.

"I drove to Monica's house the day I found out that my parents were selling the farm and I was inheriting nothing at all, and she listened as I ranted and raved. She seemed off that day, but I wasn't exactly in a happy place myself, so it was hard to say what was going on in her head. I received a small package in the mail a few days later – it was her engagement ring. She no longer loved me. I heard through the grapevine that she was dating the son of the owner of the second largest spread in Kootenai County within weeks."

Their horses slowed, and then stopped. The air was still. No bird, no insect, no breath of wind dared to disturb them.

"I thought I'd found the woman of my dreams. The woman I was going to marry. And...she was a gold digger. Once I had no money, she magically had no love."

He shrugged and smiled a small smile that didn't quite reach his eyes. "Declan was my roommate up at the U of I; he'd moved up there after he'd broken up with Iris. We were roommates for a year before he graduated."

"Do you know why he broke up with Iris?" Ivy broke in. "She never could get him to give her a straight answer."

"Nope. I didn't understand it then, and now that I've seen them together, I *really* don't understand it. They seem pretty darn perfect for each other."

Ivy grimaced. "It took me a while to change my mind on that topic," she said dryly, "but yeah, watching them together...they make a great couple. They always had. It was that fifteen-year hiatus in the middle that lost me. Iris has gone through a lot, and it makes me happy to see her find happiness again."

She drew in a deep breath and said quietly,

"I'm really sorry to hear about Monica. She sounds like a real piece of work. To lose your parents and your livelihood and your childhood sweetheart all in one fell swoop...I can't imagine."

He let out a humorless chuckle. "I'm not gonna say it was the easiest thing in the world to go through, but at least I didn't have bullies pushing me around my whole life."

"Yeah, but at least my parents are still together and if my father is cheating on my mom...well, there's literally no hope left for humanity. I think it would be more likely that Idaho disintegrates in a nuclear attack in the next five seconds than my father cheat on my mom." They both paused dramatically, waiting for the explosion, and then Ivy laughed. "See? We're both still alive."

They paused again this time, and just stared at each other for a minute. "Thanks for listening," Austin finally said. "I feel better already."

"That's what friends are for," she said with a shrug and a wink. "But to be honest, I find this part of humanity fascinating. It never fails:

When I meet someone, their life appears to be perfect. It isn't until I really get to know someone that I realize how much shit they've gone through. How much each of us wades through in life."

"When I met you at your parent's house, I thought you led a pretty perfect life," Austin agreed, chuckling. "You have great parents, a sister – I always wanted a sibling! – and this really supportive community. I had no idea what that community had done to you."

"If it makes you feel any better, pretty much no one knows what this community has done to me." They turned around and started heading back up the trail. The sun was starting to sink towards the mountains, and it wouldn't do to be out at night on this trail. "Some people knew I was miserable, but I never told anyone about the art closet incident. Not even Iris."

He looked over at her, eyes somber. "Thanks for your trust in me. It means a lot that you told me."

"Well, if I'd known you were going to try to beat me with the gold-digger story, I would've made my story more dramatic!" she said teasingly. "Always have to come out on top."

He winked. "Sometimes, I don't mind being on bottom."

She wasn't gonna lie, she wasn't quite sure she could breathe correctly after that.

CHAPTER 16

IVY

"THREE, TWO, ONE, Happy New Years!"

Declan blew on his plastic horn while Iris threw confetti in the air. Wyatt and Abby were busy tongue-dueling, Adam was discussing exercise regimens for horses with Stetson, and Austin…

Ivy looked up at him to find him staring down at her, grinning hugely, his normally bright green eyes dark with lust. "Happy New Years," he whispered, before pulling her against him. He nestled her soft body against his hard planes, and as she looked up at him, she was sure her eyes were dark with lust too. He was sex on a stick – the cutest guy she'd ever dated, by far.

And as their lips met, she mentally allowed herself to claim the idea that they were dating. Although she'd fought it originally – it was supposed to be revenge on Tiffany and Ezzy, nothing more – that had somehow disappeared.

With a groan, Austin buried his hands in her hair and tilted her head to the side so he could gain better access to her mouth. She groaned back, feeling electricity dance over her skin. She couldn't breathe; didn't want to breathe; only wanted to feel.

"My place?" Austin murmured when he'd pulled back just a hair.

"Yes please," Ivy whispered back. She knew what he was asking, and she was saying yes. Yes, with all of her heart and soul.

She'd finally realized that no Christmas miracle was coming. No New Year's Eve fairy was going to save her sorry ass. Come morning, she was going to have to tell the world everything. Come clean. Fess up.

But tonight was one last night to enjoy what

she had. No condemning looks, no yelling, no disappointment. For one last night, she could pretend to be a successful artist who was on top of the world.

She'd deal with reality in the morning.

CHAPTER 17

AUSTIN

$\mathcal{H}$E WOKE UP SLOWLY, fighting his way through the layers. He was happy. Very happy. He didn't know why, but he was.

Something soft and warm was in his bed. He snuggled closer, his dick waking up before his brain did. Hmmm…it smelled good. Like chocolate and cinnamon.

His eyes popped open. That "it" was Ivy. He'd brought her home last night and they'd made love, slow and sweet, in his bed.

Which she was still in.

Which his dick was *very* happy about, and his

brain wasn't far behind. He pushed her hair out of the way, nuzzling the back of her neck and breathing in deeply. She smelled like chocolate and cinnamon and sex, which had to be the most potent aroma in the world. He began kissing his way down her soft, white back, each kiss bringing him closer to—

"Urgh." The grunt emanated from Ivy, and made Austin chuckle to himself. He'd wondered if Ivy was a morning person, but until now, hadn't had a chance to find out for sure.

He was beginning to guess Most Definitely Not.

He began working his way back up her spine, intending to nuzzle her neck again, when she sat straight up in bed.

"Oh," she said, looking at him. Her face crumpled, and Austin watched, concerned, as a flurry of emotions crossed her face. Panic? Anger? Worry? He couldn't tell. He opened up his mouth to ask her what was wrong and then she was shooting out of bed, grabbing her clothes off the floor. "I have to go. I have to go right now. I can't be here." Her voice was trembling and her fingers didn't seem to be cooperating, because she was only managing every other button or so on her shirt.

"What's wrong?" Austin finally got in. He couldn't think of what would cause her to react this way. She'd seemed awfully happy to be in his bed last night. Was she having morning-after regrets? That couldn't be it. How could she regret such a beautiful event?

She was frantic, not focused, not making sense. "I gotta go," she said, not looking him in the eye, and then she was gone, running down the stairs, clomping on each step in her untied boots, and the front door was slamming closed and she was gone.

Austin stared at the bedroom door, still hanging ajar in her wake.

What the hell just happened here? He blinked three times, consciously and slowly, hoping to reset his brain or the world or something.

But instead, he heard the squealing of tires as Ivy tore out of his driveway in her sister's borrowed car. She'd insisted on driving to his house last night, separate from him. Had she known all along that she wouldn't want to be there come morning?

Had she *planned* to run out of the house like her ass was on fire?

He didn't know, and didn't know how to begin to find answers.

CHAPTER 18

IVY

S HE MADE IT into the parking lot of the
library before she pulled over and
began to sob. Huge, body-wracking sobs that
made it hard to breathe and she didn't know
what to do or say or go, or how to be.

She'd known this day would come. For almost a month, she'd done a mighty fine job of
ignoring reality. Between telling herself that a
Christmas miracle would come along to save her
sorry ass, and just plain being good at ignoring
what she didn't want to think about, she'd made
it through this stay in Long Valley without con-
fronting the truth.

She was stuck a thousand miles away from home, without a way to get there, and the only thing left to do was to throw herself at the mercy of her parents. She had to tell them the truth. Them and Iris and Austin.

She didn't want to. Oh, how she didn't want to. She'd spent the last month trying to figure out how to avoid *exactly this situation* and yet…she hadn't come up with a solution. Not even a partial one. Not even a really awful one.

There was no out, except with honesty. She had to admit that she was a failure in every respect. It was after midnight, her carriage had turned into a pumpkin, and there was no fairy godmother to save her.

Everyone would hate her, of course. How could they not? She'd done nothing but lie to them for years now. And Austin…he'd never forgive her. Running out on him like that; misleading him all this time. He was finally going to know the truth about her.

Everyone would.

In the midst of the waterfall of tears, the thought bubbled up to the surface that she couldn't ignore, that she couldn't reason away: Why had she become an abstract impressionism artist?

She forced herself to truly ask herself that; to get an answer for it and not just skim over it and move on like she had been.

Looking back on it, that was the biggest lie of all – the lie to herself. Truthfully, she hated the abstract movement. When she'd been sitting in the classroom, her art teachers showing the styles up on the projector, deriding plebeian art styles like landscapes, she'd nodded and followed along.

She'd wanted to fit in. It became crystal clear to her in that moment, everything clicking into place. Her whole childhood, she'd stuck out like a sore thumb. She and Long Valley just didn't get along. She'd wanted to go somewhere else, where *cool* people lived. Not these hicks who decorated with ceramic pigs. She'd wanted to be part of the "in" crowd, and be loved.

Not loved for who she was, because she hadn't really known who she was back then.

How could someone love her for her, if she didn't even know who "her" was?

But loved nonetheless. *Some* kind of love was better than scorn and ridicule and hatred and bullying. Some kind of approval was more than she'd ever gotten before.

And so she'd spent fourteen years, chasing this love and approval. All for what? So she could be living below the poverty line, struggling to eek out a living as a waitress in a diner for a boss who was a dick to her, all so she could chase the dream of doing something she didn't even want to do?

It was insanity. All of it.

The sobbing hiccups turned into tears, which eventually dried up, until all Ivy could do was stare through the foggy windshield at the side of the library, her eyes burning, her body wrung out.

It was time to go accept her punishment, and tell her family the truth. She'd start there. They loved her. They would understand, or at least not throw her out on her ass into the snowbank.

She hoped.

WAITING for Iris to show up from her mother-in-law apartment next door was probably the longest six minutes of Ivy's life. It was six minutes on the clock, but ten years in Ivy's mind.

When she'd come home from Austin's house, her mother had been frantic with worry over the blotchy face and red eyes of her younger daughter. Instead of answering her cascade of questions, Ivy had asked if Iris could come over so she could tell everyone everything at once, rather than having to repeat herself. One time was awful enough, thankyouverymuch.

Her dad had gone to fetch Iris, and the wait for them to return was slowly driving Ivy insane.

The ticking of the clock, the stares from her mom, the pacing back and forth…

It was like fingernails on a chalkboard. Ivy wasn't sure if she wanted her dad and Iris to hurry up so she could tell them and get it over with, or never, ever come home so she didn't have to admit to anything at all.

But finally, in came Dad through the front door, knocking the snow off his boots while guiding Iris in. She was staring at Ivy, a confused look on her face that clearly said, "What the hell is going on here?"

A question Ivy was about to answer. The only thing she could do was tell the truth and hope they forgave her.

When everyone settled down on the floral brocade couch that had graced the McLain's living room since the early 90s, sitting in a line, all staring at Ivy, she hopped to her feet. She couldn't just sit there. She had to walk, to pace, to get the panic and energy out of her.

She turned and looked at her family, sending them a pained smile.

"I work at the Rockstar Diner," she said. She wasn't entirely sure why she was starting there, but she needed to start somewhere and that seemed like as good of a place as any. "I am a waitress there. That's how I pay my bills. I live upstairs over my art studio – you know, that one

I love to brag about and I post pictures of all the time on Facebook? Well, the upstairs isn't actually supposed to be an apartment. It was storage for the last tenant. Other than the tiniest bathroom that you ever did see, with a sink, a mirror, and a toilet crammed into it, there's no running water. I take showers down at the local YMCA and I cook on a hot plate while sitting on my bed."

She drew in a deep breath. This next part was the worst part, and she wasn't sure which was going to happen: Getting it all out or passing out. It was going to be close.

"I never made it as an artist. Not really. Not enough to pay my bills. You can't live on a hundred dollars a month in the Bay area, and that was if I was lucky and actually sold a painting that month.

"I'm not really sure where it all started. The lying. I've spent a lot of time in my oversized-closet-turned-apartment, trying to remember how I got into this mess to begin with, and I don't know. I don't remember the first small white lie. I probably just exaggerated how much

I made on the sale of a painting. I never told you guys that I quit waitressing after I graduated from college; I just let you guys assume that I had. I know that sounds stupid, but I tried to minimize the amount of lying that I did, even if I was just assuaging my conscience by lying through omission."

Which was when the damn tears started rolling down her cheeks; hot, burning trails, dripping onto her shirt.

"I know that lying through omission isn't any better than actually saying the lies. I know better than to tell lies of any kind. Y'all raised me better than this."

She snuffled, scrubbing her face on her arm. "I wanted to be something more than I was. I wanted to rub it in the face of every person who was an ass to me in school. I wanted to prove that I was successful, and I wanted to post that proof on Facebook. The bigger the lies, the less I could back out of them and play them off as a joke. Pretty soon, everyone believed me, and I finally got that validation that I've spent my whole life craving.

"But none of it was real."

She stopped for a moment, black panic swirling around her. She wasn't done yet, and she knew the shock on her family's faces was only going to get worse. Her mother's mouth was hanging open and her dad's face had gone white. Iris was crying silently.

Ivy wanted to die. Just crawl into a hole and never come out again. But just like before, in that damn art closet at the high school, she kept going. Because she had to.

"I said that I work at Rockstar Diner, but even that was a lie. I don't. Not anymore. I got fired when I didn't come back after the party. The truth is, I can't go back. I don't have the money to. I was barely hanging on by my finger-nails, and had scraped and saved for two months to pay for the plane tickets to come home for the big shindig. When Iris fell—" their eyes met and pain flashed in Iris' deep blue eyes and Ivy felt sick for making her sister feel awful but she *had* to finish the story and get this all off her chest, "—I canceled my flight back home, but the cost to buy a new ticket…"

She shrugged. All pride was gone. The pride that had kept her going for years, pretending to be something she wasn't, had disappeared.

"I don't have it. I can't leave. I'm stuck here, until…well, I don't know. You kick me out? I'm going to lose everything – all of my paintings, my clothes, my furniture, my art supplies… When my landlord doesn't get my rent check for January, he's gonna start the proceedings, and eventually get me evicted. He'll sell my stuff, and meanwhile, I'll still be here. Living in my childhood bedroom and hiding from the world."

She broke down into hiccuping sobs then, harder, deeper, even more painful than the tears in the car had been.

But as awful as it felt, it also felt cathartic. Maybe her family would hate her, disown her, throw her out on her ear. But at least she wasn't lying to them anymore.

She hadn't realized how hard it'd been to hide the truth from them all this time. To pretend that everything was fine, when it hadn't been.

Maybe telling the truth was awful, but hiding the truth? That was even worse.

She felt her mom's arms wrap around her, pulling her against her soft chest, whispering in her ear. Ivy couldn't hear the words over the pain pouring out of her, but she knew they were loving words. Sweet words.

Words of forgiveness.

"I'm—I—I'm so—so—so sorryyyyyyyy!" Ivy wailed. "I didn't wa—want to disappoint yoooouuuuuuuu…" Her shoulders were shaking, her body was shaking and she couldn't breathe and she couldn't talk. Her mom's arms stroked down her back and hair as she whispered in Ivy's ear and then, her dad was there, on the other side. Her dad, who was *not* an emotional man. Who had not been raised to hug his daughters or tell them that he loved them. He was holding her and he too was shaking.

Finally, Ivy's sobs died down just enough that she could hear her father. "I'm sorry, I'm so sorry," he was whispering.

"Sorry?" Ivy choked out, the endless cascade of tears ever falling, burning her eyes, burning her cheeks. "For what? For raising a daughter who lies?"

"For not standing up to those girls at your high school."

Ivy froze. She remembered. All of it came rushing back. After all this time, she remembered where the lies had started, and now that she remembered, she was shocked she'd ever forgotten. It was the day that Tiffany and Fredrick announced their engagement on Facebook.

Fredrick had been her one and only boyfriend in high school. It'd been a pretty innocent relationship – some kisses, some snuggling together during football games. And then, they were discovered together – Tiffany and Fredrick under the bleachers, making out, when he was supposed to be meeting Ivy for the game. It was the fall of their senior year, and it had broken Ivy's heart.

Years later, and Tiffany and Fredrick were getting married. Posting adorable pictures of themselves on Facebook. Showing off a rock the size of Kansas on her ring finger. Everything Ivy had wanted in life.

They never did end up getting married, iron-ically enough. He was caught cheating on Tiffany with the gas station attendant for Mr. Petrol's. Which was a sick kind of justice in Ivy's mind.

But that night of the engagement-fest, Ivy posted about an art show she'd been invited to on Facebook. She'd been so far down the totem pole in terms of popularity and star power, the hosting art gallery hadn't even bothered to put her on the ad-vertisements for the show. So Ivy had made up her own flyers, posting them on Facebook for all to see.

She told herself that it wasn't really a lie – after all, she *was* going to be at that show. She was just making advertisements that reflected that – fixing the oversight of the art gallery.

It was *possible* that she'd made her name rather large on the hand bill. Perhaps even added a few stars around her name. Of course she would, right? She was the one designing the flyers. She could pretty them up however she wanted.

Even as she was designing the flyer, she'd felt

guilt eating away at her stomach. She hadn't known then that it would be her constant companion for years to come.

Ivy pulled back, looking at each person in turn. Each person that she loved dearly. "I lied to you, I lied to the world, and sometimes, I even managed to lie to myself. I'm sorry. I'm sorry I let you down." Her throat choked up again but she swallowed hard, pushing the lump down, continuing on. "Truthfully, I need to forgive Tiffany, Ezzy, Fredrick, and everyone else in high school who tried to make me miserable. Who *did* make me miserable. Hating them has only made me hate myself, and do things that I never should have."

She took a deep, cleansing breath as her mom rubbed her back in small circles, occasionally patting her comfortingly. Ivy almost felt like she should let out a large, satisfying burp so her mom would stop trying to burp her, but that thought only made her smile.

Smiling. How lovely it was to smile.

She looked up and caught Iris' eye, who was

also grinning. "What?" she asked, confused. "Why are you smiling?"

At that, Iris let out a laugh. "Because! You say that *I'm* stubborn! You're taking it to a whole new level!"

Ivy narrowed her eyes at her sister. "At least I'm not working myself into a state of blindness," she informed her tartly.

"At least I'm not practically homeless!" Iris retorted.

"I just don't understand where you two get that from," Mom declared. "You both are just bone-headed."

Dad let out a snort.

Mom turned on him, jabbing her hands onto her hips and glaring. "And just what was *that* supposed to mean?" she demanded.

Dad's snort turned into a chuckle. "You don't know where our darling daughters got their stubbornness from? Have you met you?"

Ivy was the first to start laughing. Maybe it was the relief of finally telling her family the truth, and not having them hate her. Maybe she'd finally snapped. Gone 'round the bend.

But whatever it was, she couldn't help herself. She bent over, sides aching, laughter spilling out of her. Iris and Dad joined in, and then even Mom was laughing. They held each other up as the laughter filled the room.

Moments, minutes, hours later – Ivy couldn't tell any longer – they finally straightened up as the laughter died away. Mom gave Ivy a huge hug. "I'm proud of you for telling us the truth, dear. I won't lie and say I'm happy to hear that you've been hiding so much from us for so long, but I'm glad you came clean. I have to ask: Does any of this have to do with a certain handsome extension agent?"

Ivy shook her head quickly, paused, and then slowly nodded. "I…uhhh…woke up this morning next to him—" her face flamed red at the idea of discussing her sex life with her parents and she hurried on before her mom could bring up birth control or the birds and the bees or something else equally as mortifying, "—and time had run out. I'd been telling myself ever since Iris fell that I'd deal with this later. After Christmas. After New Year's. I knew at some point, y'all would notice that I took up residence here and hadn't moved back out again, but I kept hoping a miracle would hit. Not only that, but…"

She took another deep, cleansing breath. "I don't like abstract art." *Whoosh*. The stress and anxiety she'd been feeling for years disappeared.

She'd never said those words out loud. She'd never let herself think those words. Not so bluntly. Not so forcefully.

But it was true.

Her dad grinned at her. "Damn girl, I'm glad to hear that," he said with a chuckle. "I never could get into it. You are so talented, but that shit just looked like a drunk man splashing paint everywhere."

Ivy let out a snort of laughter at that. "Oh Dad," she said, wiping her tears of happiness and pain away, "I love you."

He turned red and mumbled something that could've been, "I love you too," or "Roses are blue," or "I go *achoo*." Ivy was pretty sure it was the first option, although with her dad, it was never a guarantee.

"I'm not sure what I'm going to do now," Ivy admitted with a shrug. It was freeing to say. The shackles were falling off. She didn't know what she was doing or where she was going with her life, but she did know that she felt like she could *fly*. "Truthfully, I was working hard as a waitress so I could pursue my dreams of painting abstract impressionism, and I don't even like it! Is 32 too young to have a midlife crisis?"

Her dad patted her on the arm. "Your mom and I can help you. We can pay for a plane ticket back down to California, and we can lend you some money. We just want you…well, you know, it's important that…" He gulped, looking uncomfortable.

Emotions – John McLain's Least Favorite Thing in the World.

Her mom gracefully jumped in, saving her husband just like she'd been doing for the past 40 years. "What your dad is trying to say, dear, is that we just want you to be happy. If that's down in California, putting together sculptures with used pop cans, or living in your old bedroom and waitressing down at Betty's Diner, your happiness is what matters."

"Considering Tiffany works at Betty's, I'm pretty sure I'm going to skip that second option," Ivy said, wrinkling her nose.

"Fair enough," her mom said with a chuckle. "Is there another kind of art you'd rather do than abstract? You could always paint handsome cowboys, you know. I'm pretty sure there's at least one cowboy who'd be willing to sit for a portrait." She winked at Ivy.

Ivy stared at her mom.

"What?" her mom asked blankly. "If you don't like the idea, you don't have to—"

"Oh Mom, you're a genius!" Ivy said, throwing her arms around her mom and hugging her ecstatically. "This is perfect!"

She ran down the hallway, wings on her feet, leaving her bemused family behind her.

She had work to do.

CHAPTER 19

AUSTIN

$\mathcal{A}$USTIN STARED AT HIS BOOK, the words swimming around, chasing each other on the page. It had been − he looked at his watch − 58 hours since Ivy had run out of his house like her ass was on fire, and he was no closer to understanding what had happened now than he was when it had happened.

Girls. You can't live with them, and you can't live without 'em.

Well, actually, that wasn't true. He'd lived without them for years. He could totally live without them again. In fact, he'd fully planned on living without them. Ivy had just been a slight deviation in those plans, but that phase was behind him. He'd learned his lesson. No girls ever.

Except for horses. Bob needed a girlfriend.

Oh, and Austin should get a dog. What red-blooded cowboy living in the mountains of Idaho didn't have a dog? He could adopt one. Michelle Winthrop down at the pound was always trying to get pets into a good home. He should drive down and pick one out. A male one, though. Just to be on the safe side.

He glanced at his watch again. Dammit. The pound closed an hour ago.

Well, he'd go tomorrow on his lunch break and bring home a companion. Someone to love him and hang out with him and keep his bed warm at night.

He groaned. He didn't want a damn dog to keep his bed warm. He wanted a woman. Ivy McLain, to be exact.

Hmmm…does she have a middle name? Austin paused, trying to remember if he'd ever heard either way.

He shook off the thought. Never mind that.

New plan: He was going to drive to the

McLain household and he was going to demand to see Ivy and he was going to talk some sense into her, and maybe tie her to a chair until she told him what was going on in that thick, stubborn, beautiful head of hers.

Much better than snuggling up to a smelly, farting male dog that would hump every leg within ten miles.

He tossed his book aside and strode over to his elk antler coat rack, grabbing his jacket off one of the tines. He shoved it on, muttering as he grabbed his keys and wallet. He was done sitting around and wondering what went wrong. He was going to demand some answers. He was going to demand she tell him why she ran off on him the other day. He was going to demand that she tell him if she loved him, because he sure loved—

He yanked the front door open and almost barreled over Ivy.

"Oof!" he gasped, all of the wind forced out of his lungs at the impact. Instinctively, he reached out and grabbed her, yanking her to him, keeping her from falling backwards off the front porch.

They froze, arms and legs tangled together, bodies pressed tight, staring at each other, half suspended in the air, until a snowflake drifted down and landed perfectly on the tip of her nose. She huffed her breath out, trying to blow the flake off.

The small puff of air broke the spell surrounding them, and he quickly straightened up, taking a step back from her. He needed some breathing room. He needed to gather his thoughts.

He needed to say something.

Their collision had knocked more than the air out of his lungs; it had knocked all of the self-righteous anger out of his brain, too, leaving him with nothing but a big blank.

Talking to Ivy was a lot easier in theory than in practice.

He glanced down and noticed the smallish flat package in her hands and latched onto it with both hands. Figuratively, of course.

"Wanna share with the class?" he drawled,

looking down at the brown-wrapped package and then back up at Ivy's flushed face.

"Can I come in?" she asked. "Or were… were you going somewhere?" Her eyes flicked down to the keys he had clutched in his hand. Another lazy snowflake drifted down, landing on her right eyelid. She fluttered her lashes, trying to get the offending frozen liquid out of her eye, and Austin gently wiped it away, his frustration and anger gone as quickly as the snowflake disappeared.

The tension that had been roiling around in his stomach like a volcano about to erupt disappeared. He felt calmer already. Being around Ivy did that to a guy. Or at least to him.

"I was coming to talk to you," he admitted with a pained grin. "C'mon in." He stepped to the side to let her in, a trail of chocolate and cinnamon coming in behind her, and he shut the door, stopping the cold and snow from swirling in, too. "How do you always smell like cinnamon and chocolate?" he asked abruptly, as he shrugged out of his jacket. He hung it back up on the antler rack and swung back to look at her. She was staring at him, her mouth agape.

"Never mind," he said, the tips of his ears growing warm. He hadn't meant to blurt that out. "What's in your hands?"

"This?" she said blankly, as if surprised to see it in her hands. "Oh yes, this! It's your present. Christmas present." She shoved it at him.

He took it, staring down at it for a moment, confused. "Either you're a little late or a whole lot early," he said dryly. He looked up, catching her chewing on her lower lip worriedly.

"A little bit of both," she said with a wry smile, trying to pretend as if she wasn't about ready to jump out of her skin, and failing quite miserably.

"Let's go sit down. It's warmer over on the couch anyway." To be honest, *anywhere* in the house was warmer than by the drafty old front door. He'd kept meaning to replace it before winter had hit, but somehow hadn't gotten around to it. There were slices of Swiss cheese that let less air through than his front door did.

He helped her out of her thin jacket, hanging it up beside his, which somehow looked a lot better than it really had any right to, and guided her towards his leather sofa snuggled up close to the fireplace. He thought about starting a fire to warm her up, but decided that a throw blanket would be faster.

And anyway, he wanted to know what was in the package in his hands. His curiosity was growing by leaps and bounds.

Once she was settled on the couch, a throw blanket over her lap, she was back to biting her lip again. He felt himself harden at the sight, and shifted uncomfortably on the couch next to her. He couldn't get too far ahead of himself. For all he knew, this was a "So long, and thanks for all the kisses" kind of present.

He flipped the package over slowly, and slid his finger under the tape, teasing the paper apart. He pulled the paper away to reveal…a cream-colored canvas?

"Turn it over," she said, just as he spotted a bit of wood at the edge. Oh. Duh. He was looking at the backside of an art canvas. He pulled it the rest of the way out of the wrapping and flipped it over.

His breath caught as he stared down at it. It was the Goldfork Mountains in all their majestic glory, streaks of color emanating from behind the jagged peaks so vivid and real, he thought he could reach out to touch the sky.

"Oh Ivy," he murmured, and then his gaze drifted down from that magnificent sky to a cowboy on a horse, looking towards the setting sun, rays of light striking his cheeks.

Not *a* cowboy. Him. She'd painted him on Bob.

"Oh Ivy," he repeated, stunned, his eyes taking in the tiniest details that she'd managed to capture. The way his hair curled at his nape. The light scar above his eyebrow where he'd fallen and taken a header against a bedpost as a toddler. Even the way he held his shoulders.

It was him.

"You painted me," he said quietly. "I saw this when you'd first started working on it, of course, but I wasn't in it before. Why did you..." He trailed off when the tears started rolling down her cheeks.

"I hate crying," she announced with a wobbly smile. "It gives me a headache, and makes my skin all blotchy and red, and I've never figured out how to cry in a pretty way. I always look like a disaster zone when I do it." She sniffled through her tears, sending him a self-deprecating grin.

He jumped up and grabbed a box of Kleenexes and brought them back for her. She took one, blowing her nose into the tissue gratefully. He didn't think she looked like a disaster zone, although it was true that her eyes were pretty red. Somehow, she made even that look beautiful, though.

He decided that arguing with her wasn't going to do him any good, and kept his trap shut, waiting for her to go on.

"I've hated this painting ever since I started it. I mean, I loved it because it was beautiful and fun to paint, but I felt like I was betraying my training. I went to college to learn what a *real* artist paints. Recreating a scene in front of you was cheating. Hell, a camera can do that.

"But Austin?" She paused for a moment, wiping at her cheeks again. "I love this painting more than anything I've ever done in my life."

It all came tumbling out then, like the rushing of the river when the canyon walls squeezed it tight, forcing it to shoot out the other side. She wasn't making it as an artist in San Francisco. She'd lied to him, she'd lied to everyone, because she'd wanted to pretend that she'd succeeded.

He remembered back to the art closet and the boyfriend at the high school football game as she talked. The times she'd been shoved into a closet, or into a toilet. He understood wanting to prove to them all that she could make it as a painter, but...

"Why did you lie to *me*?" he asked quietly, the hurt bleeding out in his voice. "I understand lying to your classmates – I mean, it's not the best thing ever, but I get it. But why me? Did you think you had to pretend to be someone else to make me like you?"

Her blue eyes looked at him, haunted. "I shouldn't have. I didn't mean to. I didn't say to myself, 'I'm going to lie to Austin about who I am.' I had just been telling people stories of my success for so long, I didn't think there was any way to stop. I couldn't confess to you, but not tell my family, you know? You would let it slip to Declan, who would tell Iris, who would tell my parents, who would lecture me on disappointing them and making poor life choices. I had to tell everyone the truth, or no one at all. If it makes you feel any better, I've been lying for a lot longer than I've known you."

He smiled a little at that. Just a little. His heart squeezed with the pain of betrayal as his eyes drifted back down to her painting, looking at every stroke of color, bursting from the canvas.

She was so damn talented. And such a damn liar.

"So tell me: Why did you run out of here the other day like your ass was on fire? Why are you telling me all of this? Why not go back to California and continue to lead your fake, perfect life where you're the next Jackson Pollock?"

She flinched like he'd struck her. "I deserved that. And also, kudos for knowing Pollock. I'm impressed."

He smiled again, just the tips of his mouth curving up and then disappearing as he stared at her intently, waiting for her to explain. He was surprised by how betrayed he felt by her. It wasn't like he'd known her for years. He'd only met her the month before. But he'd trusted her.

Just like he'd trusted Monica and his parents. *Oh.*

It made sense. Of course. To have someone break his trust by hiding the truth from him? That was the one chink in the armor around his heart. The pieces fell into place – Monica lying so she could marry rich and lord over everyone that her husband was the biggest farmer in town. His dad lying to his mom and him, about loving either of them. His parents lying to him about loving him more than they loved to hurt each other.

Honestly, he wasn't sure if there was anything Ivy could've done to hurt him more.

"I don't have the money to go back," she admitted in a small voice. "When I canceled my return flight after Iris fell, I had expected to pay a small fee to reschedule the flight. I could've handled that. But the 'small fee' ended up being almost as much as a whole new ticket. I really had to save and struggle for months to pay for the first ticket. I couldn't pay for it twice.

"I knew that this whole time." He flinched. She was admitting to intentionally lying to him, and also admitting that she was only fessing up because she had to. He felt a little sick. "I just kept hoping some miracle would come along and save me. I didn't know what, but I figured hey, it was Christmas, right? So *something* could happen. Maybe I have a fairy godmother who has thus far been hiding herself from me, who pops out of my stocking and bops me on the head." He chuckled a little at that, and then somehow hated her all the more for making him laugh. He didn't want to laugh. He was pissed.

"New Year's Day, it all came tumbling down.

The hope that this would somehow just go away, the stupidity of thinking that a bunch of money would magically appear in my bank account... I'd told myself that I'd tackle this problem after the new year. Well, it was New Year's morning, and I had no idea what to do. So I ran."

The silence between them stretched out. He didn't know what to do or say. After Monica, it'd been such a leap of faith to trust a woman again. Her sense of humor, her laugh, her talents, her intelligence, her beauty...he'd let his heart do what he'd known he shouldn't have.

He was such an idiot.

Sensing she was losing him, the words began spilling out faster. "I've always fought doing landscapes, but *especially* landscapes of Idaho. I hated this place and never wanted to think about it again. I did this one because they were there, and I wanted something easy, but I hated it from the get-go. It wasn't right. No matter what I did to the sunset or the mountain range itself or the pine trees, it wasn't right. And then I realized – it's because I needed you in it. Idaho without Austin isn't an Idaho I want any part of."

It stung. It stung because it was exactly what he wanted to hear, and yet, now…it was tarnished. How could he trust her?

His throat closed a little, which just made him angry. He'd only cried once as an adult, and it was the day his parent's divorce was finalized. He hadn't even cried over Monica Gold Digger Klaunche.

He wasn't about to cry over a girl he'd only met a month ago.

Not

Happening

The anger at her betrayal, her lies, welled up in him. At the fact that he cared so damn much about what she chose to do with her life. None of it mattered to him. Not anymore.

"Thanks for the painting," he gritted out, past the lump in his throat that only seemed to be growing exponentially, dammit. "I'll be sure to treasure it always. You can leave now."

Her expression broke his heart. She smiled tremulously, always trying to put a brave face on things, and said quietly, "I deserve that. Every bit of that. I've done nothing to earn your trust, and everything to break it. I love you, Austin Bishop. And if you ever decide to give me a second chance, I'll be waiting for you."

She stood up then, hurrying to the front door, drawing on her coat, disappearing into the darkness and cold, leaving a heartbroken shell of a man behind.

CHAPTER 20

AUSTIN

MARCH, 2018

*H*E OFFICIALLY HATED WINTER.

He didn't used to. He used to like sledding and walks in snowstorms and ice skating with beautiful red—

Not going down that road.

"C'mon, Chip," he said, tugging at his chocolate lab's leash. She'd started sniffing at a trashcan, no doubt hoping she'd be able to knock it over and eat whatever was inside.

She was this ball of brown fur and pink tongue, always busy, always moving. He'd adopted a lab so she could help him when he went birding, retrieving ducks and geese out in the field.

He'd adopted a *female* chocolate lab because she just had so much personality. She was more lovable than all of the other puppy dogs in the litter combined together. A female dog wouldn't hump people's legs, another bonus in his mind, although the jury was still out on whether Chip let one rip whenever she felt like it.

He hadn't decided yet if he loved having a dog in his life for the companionship, or hated her for making him laugh. He'd already lived through another female in his life who'd made him laugh despite her destroying his life around him, although he had to give it to Chip: At least she only chewed up couch legs. She didn't chew up and spit out his heart.

Which was an improvement.

Probably.

Although his leather couch was starting to look a little worse for the wear.

He spotted Once Upon a Trinket, a stationery/gift shop at the corner of Main and

Second and started tugging Chip towards it. He'd taken to loading Chip up into the truck and driving her all the way to Franklin to go for walks, because Franklin reminded him less of that...*other* woman. It wasn't quite as painful to walk around in it, although he was studious about avoiding the street where the ice skating rink was located. He wasn't sure if he would ever put on another pair of skates.

"Stay out here, girl," Austin said gruffly, tying her leash to the bench outside the front door. "I'll be right back."

His secretary's birthday was coming up next Monday, something she'd been sure to repeatedly "casually" mention to him about 73 times per day. He was sure if he didn't get her a card and a box of chocolates, she'd leave for lunch and never be seen again.

Like some other females he knew.

Of course, he was happy about that. He wanted it, in fact. Had demanded that it happen.

He pushed the front door open, the tinkling bell alerting the clerk at the checkout counter to his presence. "Hi!" the girl said, all chipper and friendly.

Austin hated her already.

"Do you have birthday cards?" he grunted.

"Oh sure, right back this way!" she said, heading to the back of the store. He watched her hips sway slightly as she walked, trying to drum up some sort of enthusiasm for the sight, but found himself yawning instead.

Literally yawning.

Well, it was a good thing he hated her, right?

"Down this side and halfway up the other," the gal said when they stopped at the end of an aisle. She sent him a bright smile, and then froze. She stared at him in shock.

"What?" he growled.

"Nothing. Nothing." She sent him another smile, this one overly bright, and scurried back up to the front of the store.

With a grunt, he headed down the aisle, picking up and putting down cards at random. He needed a nice card, without being overly sentimental – this was his 53-year-old-going-on-54-year-old secretary, not his girlfriend or his mother – but also not crude. There were a few cards that made him blush, and he shoved those back quickly. He glanced up front, hoping the clerk hadn't been able to spot what he'd just picked up, and caught her staring at him again. She quickly whipped her head away, picking up a piece of paper and studying it carefully.

He was pretty sure it was blank.

He wandered further down the aisle. He had to hurry. Chip would be getting cold, out in the blustery, winter air. He grabbed another card at random. A yellow rose, simple wording…it was perfect.

He'd have them put together a box of hand-made chocolates out of the chocolate case up-front, and be set to go. He was rather proud of himself, really. In, out, and on his way. Mission accomplished.

He had the clerk put together a small box of chocolates for him, making sure to get all white chocolate ones since that was his secretary's favorite, but the gal kept sneaking glances at him.

"What?!" he barked. "Do I have something

on my face?" He scrubbed his hands across it, trying to knock the offending dirt off.

"No! I...I'm sorry. I just...I never expected to meet you."

He cocked an eyebrow at her. He was an extension agent for Long Valley County, not a rockstar.

"I didn't know you were real, actually."

Okay, this was only getting more strange.

"She did such a good job of painting you, though. Wow. I knew she was talented, but seeing you in real life...it's kinda creepy."

His eyes went wide. *She.*

There was only one *she* he could think of who would be painting him.

"Paintings?" he got out. It was all he could manage.

"Yeah. Over there." She pointed up at the front, at a huge display of oil paintings. How had he missed it on his way in? It was large and colorful and full of life and...

And full of him.

He left his purchases on the counter, forgotten. He walked over to the display, with a large placard off to the side, a smiling picture of Ivy beaming out at him. *Long Valley artist…recently moved back home…local scenery…*

He looked at the paintings spread out in front of him in a daze, taking in colors and mountains and a black bear in a stream, and a cowboy.

Him.

On a horse.

Kneeling by a mountain stream.

Smiling out at the world. Looking sternly at the world. Closing his eyes and sleeping.

He wasn't in every painting, but he was in most.

After he'd thrown Ivy out that day, or rather, she'd run out on him after he told her to, he'd told Declan that they weren't an item anymore, and he'd appreciate not talking about it. Declan had given him one of those one-armed hugs that men gave each other when trying to console each other without actually losing their dignity, and told him that he understood. Ivy's name hadn't crossed Declan's lips since. Or Austin's.

He'd thought she'd left. He'd thought she

was headed back to California, back to trying it again. She hated Long Valley, she hated Idaho, she hated the cold, she hated the truth.

She couldn't handle living in Long Valley.

And yet, here she was.

"How often does this...uhhh...Ivy McLain come in?" he asked loudly, trying to project his voice across the room to the clerk without actually having to look away from the paintings. Maybe she just dropped all of the paintings off and then disappeared to California. Or had them shipped up here. It was possible. Just because her paintings were here didn't mean she was.

"About once a week to drop off another painting." The girl was at his elbow when she said that, and he jumped. He hadn't heard her move. "I didn't know someone could paint so quickly, especially not at such a high quality. She must spend all day, every day, on these. Do you know her?"

He nodded slowly. "Yes and no," he said softly. Yes, he knew her name and how she liked her coffee and how she wrinkled her nose when she was trying to be tactful, but no, he didn't know her. Hadn't believed she could lie so thoroughly and so completely about who she was, to everyone in her life.

"Well, next time you see her, tell her how talented she is. We try to talk to her when she comes in, but she never seems to hear what we're telling her. She's a quiet one."

Ivy? Quiet? If he'd had to pick a hundred adjectives to describe her, quiet wouldn't have been on the list. She was vivacious and friendly and funny and smart and thoughtful and...a damn liar.

"I don't know what's going on between you two, but whatever's going on in her life, it's tearing her apart. I don't know her, so maybe I'm wrong in this, but look at the picture of her, smiling." She gestured at the large advertisement set in the midst of the paintings. "I've never seen her do it. If I wasn't looking at this with my own eyes, I wouldn't believe she knew how to smile."

Not...

His brain stopped. Broke. Quit processing. An Ivy who didn't smile wasn't Ivy.

In a cloud of doubt and hurt and pain and surprise, he spun around and headed to the front door. He had to get outside. Get some fresh air into his lungs.

"Hey, you forgot your stu—"

The door closed behind him, cutting off her words. Austin didn't care right then. His secretary would have to go without this year. He needed to grab Chip and go home. Maybe inside the four walls of his house, the world would start making sense again.

CHAPTER 21

IVY

S HE DIPPED THE BRUSH back into the oil paint and then rubbed her eyes with the back of her hands. A blob of paint dropped to the ground.

Whoops.

After the first dozen paint splatters on her bedroom carpet, her mother had not-so-tactfully suggested that working over a drop cloth might be a good idea, and then made her lay one down before she'd allowed her to continue working on her paintings.

Well, at least it kept Ivy from feeling guilty

every time paint splattered on the floor. That was good, right?

She shoved her frizzled hair out of her eyes. She needed to get the line of Bob's neck just right. It looked droopy right now. Bob's neck did not droop. Clenching her tongue between her teeth, she began working on the neckline. This one would be due at Once Upon a Trinket in just a couple of days, and she still had a long ways to go. She'd screwed up when she'd first started painting it; the look on Austin's face hadn't been quite right. It was his eyebrows, she'd finally figured out. They hadn't been thick enough. They were perfect now.

In the distance, she heard a knock on the front door, and then the muffled sound of her mother's voice.

Yes, she lived at home with her parents. It was embarrassing, when she took the time to think about it. She mostly tried not to, hence the frenetic pace of her work.

Well, that and so she didn't think too much about how she'd messed everything up.

It would take a while to build up her family's

trust in her again. Ivy didn't blame them; she deserved their questions and probing, every bit of it and more. At least they were letting her try to win their confidence again. Aus—

No.

She wasn't going to focus on that. She couldn't control the actions of others; she could only control her own. That was one of the biggest lessons she'd taken away from her counseling sessions so far, courtesy of her parents. She was starting to get over the pain and hurt that she'd been carrying for years, and was starting to realize that by focusing so much of her life on Tiffany and Ezzy and Fredrick, she was giving them power over her.

All she could focus on was making herself a better person. In the end, that was what mattered.

"Ivy?" her mom called through her bedroom door.

"Yeah?" she said, distracted. Bob's neck still wasn't quite right. She wasn't sure why she hated it, but she did. She'd just have to keep staring at it. It'd come to her.

"Someone's here to see you," came her mom's muffled reply.

That pulled Ivy out of her staring contest with her canvas. See her? Who would be coming to see her? She hadn't made friends when she was here in school, and nothing had changed since she'd moved back. Iris was her only friend, and her mom sure as hell wouldn't announce her like this.

She carefully laid the paintbrush down and sidled around her bed. After moving all of her art supplies up from the Bay area, her childhood bedroom had become quite crowded. Thankfully, she was used to living in small spaces. Just a few more months of steady sales, and she'd have enough to pay first and last month's rent, plus a cleaning deposit, on a small apartment of her own. Turns out, tourists visiting the area loved buying her paintings and bringing them back home with them, so as to not lose their little slice of Long Valley.

This time, her independence would be paid for by her paintings. Not a lie in sight.

If she wasn't so damn tired all the time, she'd be more jubilant at the idea.

She pulled her bedroom door open. "I'm almos—oh!" she squeaked.

Why was Austin standing there in her bedroom doorway? His eyes swept up and down her, taking in her appearance, but she was too flustered to care. She was a disaster – she probably had paint in her hair and on her nose – but whatever; she was too busy drinking in Austin. Did he have a few more wrinkles around his eyes? He looked tired. Haggard. Like he'd aged ten years in three months.

Her mom disappeared, murmuring something, but Ivy didn't hear her. Everything had narrowed down to just Austin, the rest of the world disappearing.

Wordlessly, she stepped back and let him in, and then closed the door behind him. He stood there, unsure of where to go. There wasn't much room in her overstuffed bedroom. She finally gestured to the end of the bed. "Take a seat," she rasped. She cleared her throat.

She could talk. She could totally talk.

She crawled past him and up onto the bed itself, sitting cross-legged in the middle of it. Austin had taken his cowboy hat off and was moving it restlessly in his hands, twirling it endlessly as he looked around her bedroom.

She wanted to demand what the hell he was doing in her bedroom, but decided to keep quiet for a moment. She'd let him talk when he was ready.

The silence stretched out between them like a rubber band, the tension growing stronger, and she stared at him, losing her resolve to keep quiet. If he was just coming in to stare at her walls, he could just leave again.

"I saw your paintings," he said quietly. Finally.

Although, as soon as he said the words, she wished he'd take them back. A small part of her had known that he might see her paintings someday, but since she'd planned on never seeing him again, that had been perfectly fine… in theory.

But now that he was sitting in front of her, the whole thing was embarrassing as could be. It was like those awful dreams where you're naked at school and everyone is laughing at you.

Having him see those paintings, a physical and obvious sign of how much she still loved him…

Her soul felt naked.

"I'm sorry if you didn't like—"

He held up a hand, stopping her. "Not like them?" he finished for her. He smiled for a moment at that. "You're amazing. Ivy McLain – hold on, do you have a middle name?"

Slowly, she nodded.

"Which is…?"

"Green," she whispered.

"Green. Your parents named you Ivy Green."

She nodded. It wasn't something she'd ever admitted out loud to anyone, ever, in the history of humanity. She'd planned on taking that one to her grave. She'd long ago stopped even writing a middle initial when filling out official paperwork.

But she'd lied enough to Austin. She couldn't lie again.

"What's Iris' middle name — Blue?" he asked, laughing.

"Ummm…yes?" Ivy said.

"Oh Lordy!" Austin said with a shout of laughter. He dropped his cowboy hat onto the bed beside him so he could wipe at his eyes with both of his hands. "Your parents sure are somethin'."

"I noticed," Ivy said dryly. She waited for him — not so patiently — to straighten up and stop laughing and start talking. Finally, he did.

"Ivy *Green* McLain," he snickered a bit when he said her middle name and she glared at him and he stopped snickering and hurried on instead, "you are the most talented artist I've ever seen in my life. You make the world around you come alive. Bob, me, that bear, the mountains, the sky, the way the wind bent the wildflowers on top of the hill…I was there. I could smell and feel and taste it all. Not having you paint would be a cruel joke to play on this world."

"I'm sorry I lied to you," she whispered, her eyes filling with tears. She tried to snuffle them back. She hadn't cried in months. Three, to be exact. But having him here, close enough to touch if she was so brave, meant the world to her. She could breathe again. She could smile again.

She could cry again.

The cold, gray haze she'd pulled around herself to shield herself from the world dissipated.

"I know. It's funny — seeing those paintings at that store made me understand why you did, though."

"They did?" She stared at him, trying to understand.

"Yeah. Seeing how much talent you have — it's a part of your soul. To be surrounded by blithering idiots who couldn't see that talent and appreciate it must've slowly been driving you crazy."

"Well, I was also painting different stuff back then," she said. "Maybe I wasn't as good at—"

"You could flip paint at a canvas and it'd be beautiful," he staunchly informed her.

She cocked an eyebrow at him, mimicking one of his favorite gestures. "Have you ever considered that you might be biased?" she teased him.

"Biased? I'm not biased," he protested.

"Maybe the other people looking at my paintings weren't in love with me," she whispered, biting her lower lip and staring straight at him.

She was done hiding. She was done being scared. She would say what she thought, what she meant, what she felt. If the world couldn't handle the truth, then that was their fault, not hers.

And she was starting with Austin.

He was staring at her, hardly breathing, his heart in his eyes. "You think I'm in love with you?" he whispered softly. He began to lean towards her. Just a little. But she saw it, and she knew what it meant.

"Yes, I do," she whispered back. "I think you've loved me since I spilled that damn apple cider all over you."

He grinned, his eyes crinkling up in the corners. "I really should make you pay to dry clean that jacket," he whispered.

She felt ridiculous, whispering to him when there wasn't anyone else in the room, but she leaned forward anyway, and whispered back, "I know how to pay you back."

"You do?" he asked breathlessly.

"I do," she murmured.

Finally, finally, their lips touched, and the heat and electricity and sparks arced between them so bright and strong, she was sure they were lighting up the nighttime sky above Sawyer. Tears were rolling down her cheeks – happy tears, this time – as they murmured and kissed, wiping her tears away with the pads of his thumb, whispering that he did love her. He loved her so damn much.

"Will you move in with me?" Austin asked as they finally came up for air. "I have a lot more space at my house – you could have your own art room even. I just don't want to go home without you. Please."

She shook her head slowly, smiling slightly. "No," she whispered, her tone at odds with her answer.

"No?" he repeated, confused.

"If I do that, I'll never know if I could make it as an artist. On my own two feet. Without waitressing or my parents or you supporting me. I need to know this for me. I need to do this for me. I love you, I'll date you, and if someday you ask me, I might even marry you."

"Might?" he asked, repeating her again.

"A girl's gotta keep a guy on his toes," she said and winked. "But never again am I going to allow someone else's beliefs about me and what I should do or who I should be control me. And I'm not saying that you'd do that on purpose, but I need to know that I, Ivy Green—" she winked again, "—McLain can stand on my own two feet. And if I end up having to take a wait-ressing job, well, it'll be in Franklin—" he let out a shout of laughter, "—but you'll know it and the world will know it. I will never lie to you again."

He sobered up and stared at her for a long moment. "Thank you," and then so softly, like words floating on a summer breeze, "I believe you."

And in that moment, those words were the

sweetest she'd ever heard. She had a long ways to go to earning everyone's trust back, but she'd started the process, and that meant more to her than anything in the world.

Well, except for a handsome cowboy named Austin Bishop.

Dishing Up Love (September 2022)

Gift of Love (December 2022)

~ FIREFIGHTERS OF LONG VALLEY ~

Flames of Love

Inferno of Love

Fire and Love

Burned by Love

~ MUSIC OF LONG VALLEY ~

Strummin' Up Love (July 2019)

Melody of Love (May 2020)

Rock 'n Love (March 2021)

Rhapsody of Love (February 2022)

~ SERVICEMEN OF LONG VALLEY ~

Thankful for Love (November 2019)

Commanded to Love (August 2020)

Salute to Love (June 2021)

Harbored by Love (November 2021)

Target of Love (July 2022)

ABOUT ERIN WRIGHT

USA Today Bestselling author Erin Wright has worked every job under the sun, including library director, barista, teacher, website designer, and ranch hand helping brand cattle, before settling into the career she's always dreamed about: Author.

She still loves coffee, doesn't love the smell of cow flesh burning, and has embarked on the adventure of a lifetime, traveling the country full-time in an RV. (No one has died yet in the confined 250-square-foot space – which she considers a real win – but let's be real, next week isn't looking so good…)

Find her updates on ErinWright.net, where you can sign up for her newsletter along with the requisite pictures of Jasmine the Writing Cat, her kitty cat muse and snuggle buddy extraordinaire.

Wanna get in touch?
www.erinwright.net
erin@erinwright.net

Or reach out to Erin on your favorite social media platform:

f facebook.com/AuthorErinWright

▼ twitter.com/erinwrightlv

℗ pinterest.com/erinwrightbooks

g goodreads.com/erinwright

BB bookbub.com/profile/erin-wright

◉ instagram.com/authorerinwright

CPSIA information can be obtained
at www.ICGtesting.com
Printed in the USA
BVHW042123310820
587750BV00005B/201

9 781950 570348